THE DETAILS IN THE DESIGN

THE DETAILS IN THE DESIGN

SHANNON M. HARRIS

SAPPHIRE BOOKS

SALINAS, CALIFORNIA

The Details in the Design
Copyright © 2017 by Shannon M. Harris. All rights reserved.

ISBN - 978-1-943353-79-8

This is a work of fiction - names, characters, places, and incidents are the product of the author's imagination or are used fictitiously. Any resemblance to actual persons living or dead, business, events or locales is entirely coincidental.

All rights reserved. No part of this publication may be reproduced, distributed, or transmitted in any form or by any means, including photocopying, recording, or other electronic or mechanical methods, without written permission of the publisher.

Editor - Kaycee Hawn
Book Design - LJ Reynolds
Cover Design - Michelle Brodeur

Sapphire Books Publishing, LLC
P.O. Box 8142
Salinas, CA 93912
www.sapphirebooks.com

Printed in the United States of America
First Edition – May 2017

This and other Sapphire Books titles can be found at
www.sapphirebooks.com

The idea for this story came to me while watching a fashion movie, and there are a few women who encompasses what fashion is and they deserve a standing ovation for all their hard work.

"Style is a way to say who you are without having to speak."
-Carolina Herrera-

"I don't do fashion. I am fashion."
-Coco Chane-

"That's all."
-Miranda Priestly-

Acknowledgment

This is a shout out to all the hard work that goes into making my story a reality and the people that make it happen. Writing the story is only part of the puzzle.

Avery Michaels stared dumbstruck at her phone long after the person on the other line disconnected. When she talked to the woman at the employment offices the previous day, she hadn't expected to get a call back so quickly. The woman had originally told her it could take up to two months to find something in her preferred medium. Her passion lay with all things having to do with fashion, from the publishing aspect, to the designers, and everybody and everything in-between. At six years old, she got her hands on her first fashion magazine, and the rest was history. Nothing else had ever captured her attention, but life rarely worked out the way one intended it to.

For the past year, she had been an assistant to Todd Richards, one of the most sought after food critics in New York City. All in all, it wasn't a hard job, but the excitement wasn't there anymore. That's exactly what the employment agency promised. If she could make it as Todd's assistant, she believed she could make it at any job. His hardnosed approach almost broke her at the beginning of their working relationship, but after a few months, she had settled into her role and excelled at it. She sighed and rested her head back against the couch cushions. Not only had she gotten an interview in the fashion world, but with the one fashion house of her dreams: Catherine Davenport Designs.

"Avery." Mia, best friend extraordinaire since they were both six years old and her current roommate, stood in front of her and waved her hand in front of her face. When Avery blinked, Mia took that as a positive and sat down beside her on the couch. "What's got you so spaced out?" She pointed to her phone. "Who was that?"

Avery frowned at her when she took another bite of her ice cream. Mia was one of those women that could eat anything and never gain a pound. Avery hated her for it. She bit her lip. "That," she said, waving her phone in the air, "was the agency calling me back. I have an interview tomorrow."

Mia scrunched her nose. "So soon? Who is the interview with?" She moaned and licked her spoon clean, before dropping it in the empty ice cream container, and setting it on the coffee table. When Avery didn't answer, she asked again.

"Catherine Davenport Designs."

"Get out." Mia laughed.

"It's not funny." And it wasn't.

"Are you kidding me? This is fate. The one company you wanted to interview with and you got it. What position?"

"The assistant to her assistant."

She shrugged. "You have to start someplace."

"I know. That's not what's bothering me." She sighed and slouched down even further on the couch.

"Then what is?"

"Idon'twantmycrushtogetintheway," she mumbled.

"What? Speak slower. I couldn't make that out."

Avery squinted at her, knowing full well she understood what she'd said. "I don't want my crush to get in the way." She bit her lip. "I never thought I would interview with her company."

"Oh, that." She leaned back and plopped her feet in Avery's lap. "You may not even see her that much. If you're an assistant to her assistant, there is a possibility you won't even be in the same room as her." She rolled her eyes. "Or is that the problem? You could possibly be in the same building as her and never see her or even talk to her?"

Avery closed her eyes and sunk deeper into the couch cushions. Her obsession started six years ago. She had just turned twenty-six, and Catherine gave a speech at a gala for the performing arts about accessories through the years. Of course, she knew who Catherine's designer persona was, but until that moment, she hadn't realized how truly captivating the woman was.

From the first moment Avery laid eyes on her, she knew she was a goner, but she also knew Catherine was way out of her league. Not only was she one of the most sought after designers of the last twenty-five years, but also an accomplished businesswoman. Last year, Forbes estimated her wealth at a little over fifteen million dollars.

She picked up her iPad and turned it on, staring down at the picture. Right after Catherine's presentation, Avery searched for every bit of information on her that she could find. From magazine articles, to interviews, to blogs. There wasn't much to go on, because Catherine was notorious for not giving interviews. She pretty much stayed out of the limelight, except for certain galas and parties throughout the year to honor the charities she supported and, of course, showing at fashion week.

Her lock screen showed a picture that was taken two weeks ago at a charity event for underprivileged children. Catherine wore a long, black, off the shoulder dress, with a white bodice and long train. Her white, short hair was styled to perfection, a lock of hair kept falling in her eyes, and it suited her face perfectly. Catherine was fifty-two, gay, had twin daughters, Lincoln and Abigail, and a cat named Digger, but she tended to live a very low-key life. She'd never been married, but there had been rumors over the years of different partners, but nothing concrete. "I don't know." Just looking at her picture made her heart race.

"Look, you're thinking about this too much. Take a deep breath. Good. Now another one. Let it out. Relax. You've got this. Who in their right mind is going to say no to those soul sucking brown eyes of yours? Hmm." She grabbed the iPad from her hands and studied the picture. "You know, for a woman in her early fifties, she's hot. I would do her."

Avery snatched the iPad back and dropped it on the couch between them. "Don't be so crass."

"I am just saying it like I see it. Avery, this is good news." She wiggled her toes until Avery got the hint and started messaging her feet. "This is what you've always wanted. To work in the fashion industry."

"I don't have the job yet. The lady on the phone told me there could be upwards of twenty people interviewing for the same position." She pushed Mia's feet off, stood up, and started pacing. "I probably won't even get the job. Stupid people." She ran her hands through her short black hair. Last year, she had finally decided to cut off her long locks and surprised even herself when she looked in the mirror and didn't faint at how short it was. It was cut short, but long enough that she could run her fingers through it, and no matter how many times she did or how hard the wind was blowing, it would always fall back into place. It took a lot of getting used to, but she loved it now.

Mia jumped up suddenly and squealed. "What are you going to wear?" She ran to Avery's bedroom. Avery rolled her eyes at seeing Mia sitting in the middle of her bed with her legs crossed. Instead of joining her, she stepped inside her walk-in-closet. After rummaging around for a few minutes, she walked out and placed her picks on the bed. A pair of fitted, charcoal gray Carolina Herrera trousers, a pink, button-up Chanel top, and her rattlesnake belt she bought off Etsy.

She bit her lip then walked back to the closet, and brought back a pair of three and a half-inch, black, Vernice Prada pumps. Mia eyed everything then nodded. Avery loved fashion, but if it weren't for the inheritance her maternal grandparents left her, she wouldn't be able to afford her wardrobe. "I like it. It's classic. You should leave two buttons of the shirt undone and wear the pearl necklace your grandma gave you for Christmas."

"You're right." Avery opened her jewelry box and swapped her medical alert necklace for her medical alert bracelet, then placed her pearls on top of the dresser so she would remember to wear them. When she was eight, she found out the hard way that she was allergic to shellfish. Now anywhere she went, she wore her medical bracelet or necklace and she always carried an epi-pen in her pants pocket, and one in her bag. She scrunched up her nose. "I think I am going to take the new Michael Kors bag I got last week."

"You should." Mia stood up and searched Avery's closet, stepping out with a black sheath dress. "Can I ask why you're not wearing this?"

Avery eyed the Catherine Davenport Design and sighed. "Don't you think everybody will be wearing her designs? I didn't want it to look like I was sucking up.

Don't get me wrong, I love her clothes, but I like the choices I've made."

Mia shrugged. "I do too. I was just curious." She rehung the dress.

"I don't know why I'm getting so worked up. There's a chance I won't even get the job."

"Stay positive and after you're hired, we'll celebrate."

"Celebrate?" Avery chuckled.

"Of course. I'll call Brady. It's been awhile since all three of us caught up." She wrapped her arm around Avery's waist. "Don't we celebrate all our good fortunes?"

Avery rolled her eyes. "And our not so good fortunes."

Mia dragged her back to the living room, where she deposited her on the couch. "Yes." She nodded before plopping down beside Avery. "We will celebrate."

Avery grinned. "Tacos?"

"Tacos."

❧❧❧❧

After a restless night of sleep, Avery hopped out of bed bright and early. Her nerves had been all over the place since she received the call yesterday afternoon. She ate a simple breakfast, dressed quickly, then hailed a cab. The ride was way too short, in her opinion. Avery paid the cab driver, exited the vehicle, and joined the countless other morning New Yorkers who crowded the busy sidewalk.

She fought her way through the crowd, received her visitor pass, and stepped onto the elevator. She hadn't even been out of the apartment for thirty minutes and it already felt like she had run a marathon. She pushed the button for the fourteenth floor, and tried not to fidget the closer it climbed to its destination. C.D. Designs had occupied the entire fourteenth floor of the skyscraper for the past six years. She had read in an interview that the business had doubled its revenue from that move alone. As it neared its final stop, she took several deep breaths to calm her nerves. *She could do this.*

She exited into a brightly lit reception room that was awash in a sea of chrome, stainless steel, frosted glass, and people. Every seat was occupied and at least a dozen people were standing around, waiting. If her eyes didn't deceive her, all these people were wearing C.D. Designs in some form. After further examination, the waiting room was quite spacious, but felt cramped and claustrophobic with the number of people squeezed into the space.

She turned from the spectacle in front of her and gave her full attention to the receptionist. The middle aged, well-dressed woman, incidentally also wearing C.D. Designs, eyed her from head to toe, gave the barest hint of a smile, then accepted her resume. After writing Avery's name on a long list of candidates, she informed her to find a place to wait.

Avery wasn't sure if their system was first come first served or if they had already determined the order. After two hours and countless people being called back, she was sure it was the first option; however, her assumption was shot to hell when the six people that came in after her where called back before her.

She frowned when she noticed, out of everyone still waiting, not a one of them had looked up from their phones until their name was called. Avery refused to take her phone out. It was rude. If someone needed to talk to her that badly, they could either phone back, or leave a message. And she refused to check any of her social media accounts. There was plenty of time to do that when she returned home. What she did wish was that she had brought some snacks. The bottle of water she had thrown in her bag that morning just wasn't cutting it.

Another hour went by with person after person being called back. The receptionist, whose nametag read Hannah, would point them toward the door, inform them to walk all the way down the hallway, and the office was the last on the right. When an empty seat became available, she quickly snatched it up, and almost regretted her decision when the gentleman sitting beside her tried to start up a conversation, but he quickly got a clue when she didn't respond to any of his questions.

She fought the urge to slouch in her seat as she eyed the clock above the desk that kept taunting her with its movements. She groaned inwardly when the elevator dinged, announcing its arrival and four more people walked into the room, only for Hannah to tell them that only those still waiting would be allowed an interview. That left five people, including her.

The nerves that had eaten her up all day vanished when the last person, besides her, was called back, but they quickly returned when he came back out a few minutes later with a grimace on his face and he mouthed good luck to her as he passed by. Avery watched his exit and failed to notice the woman walking into the room.

"Ms. Michaels?" Avery nodded at the woman.

The Details in the Design 17

"We're ready for you," she said in a British accent.

Avery stood up, smoothed her shirt, and picked up her bag. "Avery, please."

The redhead didn't acknowledge her and walked out of the reception room. "Follow me." Hannah winked at her, then turned back to her computer. They walked down a long hallway that was fairly lit and at the end of the hall, they turned right and entered a huge, wide space that was littered with tables, mannequins, fabric, and shelves.

They continued toward a large glassed in office and even from their distance away, she could clearly see Catherine Davenport seated behind her desk. Once inside the office, Avery took a second to evaluate everyone, and just like every other candidate, these people also wore C.D. Designs. Good grief. It was hard not to second-guess herself when literally everyone she had seen wore Catherine's designs.

"Please have a seat," her escort said and pointed to the two chairs that were placed directly in front of Catherine's desk as she made her way around the desk to stand directly behind her boss' chair. Avery spared a moment and let her eyes wander around the immaculate space. Dozens of picture frames lined the walls, with photos ranging from who she assumed were Catherine's twins and cat, to sketches of different designs, and pictures of famous designers. The space was clutter free, sleek, and modern.

"Avery," the man seated to Catherine's right said. "I'm Camden, Catherine's assistant and the woman behind us is Beth, Catherine's second assistant."

Avery fought the urge to frown at his words. If Beth already held the position of second assistant, then what was this interview for? "It's nice to meet both of you." She would reserve her judgment until she got all the facts.

"I take it I don't have to introduce the woman next to me?" Camden grinned.

Avery could do nothing to stop the blush marring her features. "No. No introduction necessary."

"Good." Camden nodded. "From your resume, you have never worked in the fashion industry before, but from what you're wearing it is clear that you know your way around fashion."

"Thank you." Avery's heart raced when Catherine spoke and she had to lean forward to catch her softly spoken words.

"Avery, I couldn't help but notice out of everyone that was interviewed today, you are the only one who didn't wear one of my designs." Avery knew that wasn't a question so she kept her mouth shut but didn't avert her gaze from the woman in front of her. "Why?" She looked at Avery over her glasses.

"I have a rather lovely black sheath dress of yours hanging in my closet, along with several other pieces from your collections. Mia, my best friend, even asked me why I wasn't wearing it. Truth be told, it never crossed my mind to wear it. It did cross my mind that by wearing one of your designs, I would look like a suck up. It gave me a moment of pause when literally everyone around me was wearing your clothes, but it was only a moment. What I'm wearing is typical of my normal workwear. I guess I don't have a solid answer."

Catherine nodded, closed her file, and rested her hands on top of it. "I spoke to Todd Richards earlier and he didn't seem all that surprised when you put in your two weeks' notice. He stated he was surprised you hadn't left sooner. To quote him, *her passion has never lay in the food industry,* but he said you were a hard worker and willing to put in the hours to complete any task he gave you."

"I'm surprised that's all he said." Avery laughed. "We didn't exactly get along the first couple of months." Without thinking, she ran her hand through her hair, then stopped when she realized what she was doing and Catherine pursed her lips. "To be fair, I didn't hate working for him, it just seemed like every day that I was there that a little bit more of my soul died. It was time for me to move on. It surprised me to get a call from the agency after only a day of being in their system."

Catherine tilted her head and Camden frowned. "What agency?" He asked.

"The Riley Employment agency."

Catherine took her glasses off and ran the tip over her lips. "What position do you think you're interviewing for?" Her expression remained unreadable even when Beth whispered in her ear.

Now Avery felt her nerves coming back full force. What was going on? "An assistant's position."

"That spot was filled four weeks ago," Camden said. "The agency needs to update its listings." He pinched the bridge of her nose.

Avery felt her heart plummet. "Okay." Well, that sucked.

Catherine slid her glasses back on and tapped her finger on her lips. "I do have another position available, so why don't you tell me what you have to offer and why I should hire you?"

Avery griped the arms of her chair harder. What position was she applying for? "I am very good at multi-tasking and have a wide range of people skills. I'm not afraid to put myself out there to get a task completed. I am loyal, even if I don't like the job, and I will give my all, to make sure that what needs to run smoothly, runs smoothly. I am quite optimistic and I try to see the—" she paused. "I try to make the most of every day. We never know when it will be our last. Life's too short to waste it being negative." She clasped her hands in her lap and fought the urge to run her fingers through her hair again. Catherine picked up her resume, scanned it, handed it to Beth, then turned back around.

Catherine took a sip of the Starbucks cup sitting on the corner of her desk before continuing. "You've never worked in the fashion industry. Again, why should I hire you, Avery?"

Goosebumps broke out all over her body at the way her name rolled off the other woman's lips. "No, I have never worked in the industry, but my passion *is* fashion. I live and breathe it, but at the end of the day, I have bills to pay. I might live for fashion, but I also like to eat." When she first received her inheritance, her grandmother told her that the money was not to be used to pay her bills or her rent. That she would have to make her own way in life, and she didn't intend to break that promise now. Avery took a deep breath. "If I may ask, what is the position you're offering?"

Beth spoke up. "We are looking for someone to take the realms of Catherine's social media presence, including Facebook, Twitter, Instagram, a blog, and whatever else needs to be done to get her name out there, especially to let everyday people know about the new line that will be launching soon; an affordable fashion line for the everyday woman. A publicity liaison. The last man that held the job turned out to be quite an incompetent fool. We need someone who will devote all their time to growing Catherine's brand. She is well known in the fashion world, but her reach needs to extend to the middle class." The job sounded almost perfect. Too perfect. She had handled a lot of Todd's social media accounts and he seemed pleased by her efforts, but dabbling and running everything were two very different things.

"Hannah informed us that you didn't pull your phone out once when you were waiting. Why?" Catherine asked.

Avery almost chuckled. "The only time I allow myself to check my social feeds is when I get home and even then, I limit the amount of time I spend on them. I find I can accomplish a lot more when I'm not distracted. Also, I find it a bit rude. People today deem it acceptable to be on their phones all day long, even when in the company of friends, family, colleagues, or even dates." She grimaced as Catherine continued to stare at her. Avery gripped the chair handles to ground herself when her gaze remained steady. Her and her stupid crush would be the death of her.

"That's quite refreshing, Avery." As her name slipped from Catherine's lips, Avery shivered and prayed to every deity that the people in front of her didn't notice. Catherine accepted the folder Beth handed her, set it on the table, and pushed it in Avery's direction. "I felt the need to interview everyone today in case another position needed to be filled." At Avery's confused look, she went on. "You've had the job since you walked in this morning. Like I said, I talked to Todd Richards." She flicked her hand in the air.

Avery felt like the floor had disappeared beneath her chair. With shaky hands, she picked up the folder and opened it. "That's all the paperwork you need to fill out and it gives all the information about the job, what will be expected of you, as well as salary, hours, etc. Look it over and if you still want the job, bring it back tomorrow morning at eight a.m. for your first day of work," Beth said.

Avery sat stunned, before getting her bearings, picking the folder up, and sliding it into her purse. "Of course." Her nerves were shot now, but a burst of pride swirled around her at the fact that she had been their pick all day. Only a little bit of anger slipped in for being kept waiting, but she squished it down. She was offered the job and that was all that mattered. It may not have been the job she thought she was interviewing for, but it would be new and exciting and she would be in the thick of the fashion world. She stood up, turned to leave, but whirled back around. "Thank you for this opportunity."

"Avery, I would not be opposed to you wearing something from my collection occasionally." Catherine slipped her glasses off and Avery swooned a little bit more. "That's all."

On shaky legs, Avery walked back the way she had come, waved at the receptionist, and entered the elevator. After exiting onto the ground level, she returned her visitor pass, walked out the door, and onto the busy sidewalk once again. She fumbled with her phone and after three rings, Mia picked up. "Looks like we're having tacos tonight."

※ ※ ※ ※

Avery's first week at her new job flew by and even though she was thrown head first into the mess that the previous man left behind, she was enjoying the challenge. It wasn't that their social media presence was bad, but it was lacking in quite a few areas. She started out synching all their social media accounts together, making it easier for her to only post to one, instead of all of them. She figured that was obvious and mentioned it to Beth, who only rolled her eyes and told her to get back to it.

On day three, she had set up a blog, and by day five, she had Catherine's schedule down pat. She tried to tell herself it wasn't stalking, because, could it be considered stalking if they worked in the same space? She thought not.

All in all, her first week was exciting, stressful, and trying, but she wouldn't change a single thing about it. She had quickly set her routine in motion and thankfully, she got along well with almost all the other twenty-three employees. She had mentioned to Beth that it seemed like a small number to run Catherine's empire, but all she got in return was a dismissive wave. She figured that in the future, she would direct her questions to someone else.

What she would change was the fact that, although she saw Catherine every day, she had only spoken to her twice and that was for a brief amount of time. She soaked up those few minutes, but it wasn't nearly enough. It was harder than she imagined being in the same space as her and not actually communicating with her. Often she would look up from her computer and watch Catherine in her element; creating something amazing from a simple piece of fabric. More than once a day, she would pinch herself just to make sure all of this was real and not a dream she had conjured up for herself.

She looked up from her laptop and smiled

when Sybil walked up to her, carrying a familiar cup. "Here," she said, setting the cup on Avery's desk, in that devastatingly sexy southern accent. "I thought you might like this. I know I needed a pick me up."

Avery took a sip of the hot tea, laced with honey and lemon, and moaned. It was heaven and just what she needed. Sybil was a seamstress and had worked with Catherine for the past five years. On her first day, Sybil had been one of the first to welcome her and had shown her nothing but kindness. The woman was drop dead gorgeous, with long blond hair, and killer blue-gray eyes, but she knew rather quickly her and Beth were a couple when Beth walked over to them on her first day and practically pissed on Sybil's leg, virtually claiming her. She wasn't sure what the two had in common, but she guessed when it worked, it worked. "Thank you. I've only been here a week, but everyone seems to work well together." Well, except for Camden, but she would keep her thoughts on him to herself. Everybody else seemed to like him.

"We do. It's a nice place to work." She turned away when someone waved her over. "Don't work too hard, Avery." She winked at her before she walked off.

It was Friday and her plans for the weekend included, but were not limited to sleeping in, grocery shopping, possibly some laundry, sitting on the couch doing nothing, and taking Polly, her three-year-old dachshund, for as many walks as she desired. She scanned the large space, her eyes drifting to Catherine's office of their own accord and locked gazes with none other than the woman herself.

Avery loved these moments. She found herself searching out Catherine quite a few times a day, and when she wasn't in the studio working, nine times out of ten, she would catch Catherine looking back at her from her office. Avery didn't read too much into it, but it still caused her heart to flutter. She smiled, then looked back at her laptop, trying and failing to concentrate on the latest blog entry she was working on when Catherine called her name.

Catherine's voice still sent shivers down her spine, but she had somewhat learned how to control her reactions. She stood up, started walking toward her, and nodded at Camden as he walked by her. He was a hard nut to crack. Some days he was genuinely nice to her. Other days, he seemed to have a stick up his ass. She didn't think anyone could be moodier then Polly but Camden was running a close second.

Avery walked in and sat down while Catherine busied herself with her sketchpad. She couldn't help but admire the older woman. Today Catherine wore one of her signature sheath dresses in black and gold, along with her ever-present Prada pumps. Her jewelry was tasteful and simple. She kept her eyes averted, but after a few minutes chanced a glance up and was surprised to see the designer staring back at her with a hint of a smile gracing her oh so kissable lips. Good grief. How long had she been spaced out for?

Catherine tapped her pencil on top of her desktop. "It's been a busy week and I haven't had a chance to sit down and talk with you. I was wondering if you would like to have lunch with me?"

Avery blinked. "I..." Why had the ability to speak suddenly abandoned her?

"It's a yes or no question, Avery." Catherine's eyes twinkled.

Avery opened her mouth to speak when Camden strolled in without knocking and sat down in the chair beside Catherine's. If she hadn't been looking, she wouldn't have caught it, but a brief glimmer of contempt crossed Catherine's features, but after a split second, it was gone.

Camden laid his folder on top of the desk and eyed them both. "Oh, dear. I hope I'm not interrupting anything?"

"Yes," Avery blurted out and grabbed their attention. Catherine tried to hold in her smile, but failed, and Camden glared at her.

"And what, pray tell, are you yelling about?"

"Camden." Catherine spoke so low Avery had to strain to hear her. "That's enough. Just because my office door is open, does not mean you can just walk in unannounced or that it is an open invitation."

"Of course, Catherine. I am sorry." He didn't look sorry to Avery and by the look on Catherine's face, she didn't believe him either. She had learned from Sybil that Camden had worked for Catherine for the past fifteen years. He had tried and failed to make it as a fashion designer, but seemed to excel at working for Catherine. Avery wondered how much hate he festered because he couldn't hack it and Catherine could and did.

"Avery."

"Yes, Catherine."

"Be ready in fifteen minutes."

Avery grinned. "Okay." She stood up quickly and fled the office, taking sanctuary back at her own desk. Ten minutes later, Camden walked out and stopped in front of her. He tapped the folder he held in his hand on the edge of the desk.

"I wouldn't get too excited. She does this for all the new hires. Just another day at the office." He whistled and walked off.

Avery glared at his back. She had to give it to him; he was a snappy dresser, in his black skinny jeans, and Cashmere sweater, but she was confident his heart was made of stone. She didn't like him and was sure he felt the same about her.

She turned back to her laptop and the blinking cursor mocked her as the minutes ticked down before Catherine joined her at her desk and motioned for her to follow her.

After a ten-minute walk, they entered the restaurant, and were seated in a corner table near a window. They quickly gave their orders and Avery tried not to fidget, but it was hard not to, knowing who she sat across from.

"Tell me, Avery? How are you liking your new job?"

Avery took a sip of water before she answered. "I'm really enjoying it. It's a new opportunity for me and I don't plan on throwing it away."

"Good."

"It's challenging, but I enjoy working with everyone and being able to showcase your new offerings on the website. Your new line really is amazing."

"Thank you. I have enjoyed designing the pieces. Something doesn't have to cost a fortune to be well-made or high end. Every woman deserves the chance to look and feel beautiful. I hope this line will give any woman the opportunity to feel that way."

"I think it's great. Have you ever thought about designing menswear?" She knew that the line of menswear Camden had designed when they were both starting out, before he took the job as Catherine's assistant, had crashed and burned, and wanted to hear

Catherine's thoughts on the subject. She sat back when her Cesar salad was delivered along with Catherine's steak.

"I don't have an inkling for designing menswear. Lincoln has somewhat of an obsession with socks. I have tinkered with the idea of creating a line of socks. Maybe a line of backpacks and messenger bags. Possibly ties."

Avery swallowed the bite she had just taken. "That is awesome. I love socks. Every year at Christmas and on my birthday, my mom and stepdad each get me a pair. I have too many pairs to count. If I see something I like, I can't help but buy them."

"What did you get this past Christmas?"

Catherine looked genuinely interested and if she wanted to listen, Avery had no problem talking. "Well." She scrunched up her nose. "My mom got me a pair of Merino Wool socks. Please keep in mind, my stepdad's tastes in socks tends to run in the same category as mine, but the complete opposite direction of my mom's."

Catherine pushed her plate to the side after she finished eating and took a sip of her water. "Do tell."

Avery looked away only for a moment. She could feel the blush rising in her cheeks and there wasn't a thing she could do about it. "My stepdad got me a pair of Slytherin house socks."

Catherine arched her eyebrow. "I wouldn't have taken you to be sorted into Slytherin," was all Catherine said.

Avery nodded mutely, until it hit her that Catherine had fourteen-year-old daughters. Of course she knew about Harry Potter. "Are you kidding me? Slytherin is awesome." She waved her hand in the air. "I never wanted to be in Gryffindor and can you imagine being sorted into Hufflepuff?" She snickered but sobered when Catherine pursed her lips. Oh, that didn't bode well. "I mean." She sat up straighter in her chair and tried not to grimace when Catherine started to talk.

"Tell me, Avery, what is wrong with Hufflepuff?" She folded her arms on top of the table.

It always amazed her how the woman hardly ever raised her voice, but could convey so many different emotions when she spoke and the blank look on her face was new, and not something Avery wanted to see directed at her again. "Well…come on, Catherine. It's Hufflepuff. Need I say more?"

Catherine sniffed. "Avery, don't be ridiculous, there is absolutely nothing wrong with being sorted into Hufflepuff."

When Catherine's facial expression cracked a tiny bit, Avery finally got a clue. She just did stop herself from patting Catherine on the hand. "Oh, Catherine. I am so sorry."

"Whatever for?"

"You were sorted into Hufflepuff, weren't you?"

"Avery, really. There is nothing to be sorry about. I am perfectly content with Hufflepuff."

"If you say so." Never in a hundred years would she have expected to be having lunch with Catherine Davenport and discussing the merits of Hufflepuff versus Slytherin, but that's exactly what they did for the next fifteen minutes. Catherine's level of knowledge surprised Avery and she quickly concluded that Catherine was a Potterhead, her girls notwithstanding. The thought left Avery warm and fuzzy. She had never felt so comfortable with anyone in her life, and she tried not to dwell on the butterflies in her stomach, but it was hard not to when Catherine would tilt her head and smile at her, like she was doing right now.

Avery shook her head and brought her thoughts back to the conversation at hand and decided to change the subject. Catherine could discuss it all she liked, but Avery would never budge on her position. Slytherin was the way to go. "I think a line of socks and ties would go over well. I don't only collect novelty socks, but I enjoy the patterned ones and I could see you making a splash with a new bag line. Not shoes, though?"

Catherine didn't say anything about the change in subject, only pointed to her feet. "Why mess with perfection?"

Avery couldn't argue with her reasoning. "Why, indeed."

They spent the next ten minutes talking about colors and Catherine waved off her offer to pay for lunch when the check arrived. Sooner than she would have liked, they were headed back to the studio. "Thank you for lunch, Catherine. I really enjoyed it." Catherine stopped her with a hand on her arm, and Avery had to fight with her body to remain calm. Even though they were in the middle of a busy sidewalk, it felt like they were the only two people present. It took all of Avery's self-control not to grab the woman and kiss her. That would be a very bad idea, but she relished the attention Catherine bestowed upon her.

"You're quite welcome and so did I. We'll have to do it again sometime."

Avery bit her lip. "I would really like that."

Without breaking eye contact, Catherine ran her hand down Avery's arm and caressed her wrist. "I couldn't help but notice your medical I.D. bracelet. Is it something I should be aware of?" After a beat, she let go of her hand, and started walking again.

What had just happened? Avery double-timed it to catch up with her. She played back the scene that had just taken place, and hoped she didn't do something stupid, so she decided to act normally. "I'm allergic to shellfish. I almost died when I was younger. I keep an epi pen in my purse and one in my pants pocket." Usually, she would tell her employer right off the bat, but her week had been so busy she had completely forgotten about it.

Catherine looked thoughtful for a moment and the frown that marred her features vanished as quickly as it had come. "I am glad you told me. From time to time, I will cater a lunch or a dinner if we are working late, and most people usually request some type of shellfish. I will make sure, in the future, that we order something different."

Avery frowned. "No, I don't want you to go to the trouble. Not for me. If you order something separately for me, I'll be fine."

"Don't be absurd. If I am paying for it, I will order whatever I choose. If my employees want shellfish, they can do order it on their own time, and with their own money."

No one she had ever worked for before had ever shown her such compassion and that it was coming from Catherine added the cherry on top. It also had another side effect on her. It only solidified her crush even more. She was in deep trouble and she wasn't sure she wanted to dig herself out of it anytime soon. Especially since she could still feel the imprint of Catherine's fingers on her wrist. "Yes, Catherine."

Upon entering the building, Avery stayed back when Catherine stepped into the elevator. Avery wished she could see the woman's eyes, but she had on her signature sunglasses. Avery smiled and she could have sworn she caught a ghost of a smirk in return when the doors closed behind the designer. Beth didn't talk to her much, but the one thing she did say, and was quite vocal about, was the fact that Catherine rode the elevator alone. No exceptions. Avery could respect that. That way it would make it so much sweeter when Catherine finally did invite her along for the ride.

On Tuesday, she got another invitation to lunch and even though they stuck to safe topics, Avery still enjoyed her time with Catherine immensely. There were still little touches here and there, but as she had observed Catherine the previous day, her boss tended to give simple touches to a lot of her employees. Then the doubts came. At best, they had a tentative friendship, nothing more, and Avery had to try and not become any more invested than she already was. They had agreed to lunch on Wednesday, but that never happened and they weren't able to spend any one-on-one time together for the rest of the week. She cared for Catherine, but was it worth losing her job over?

Later that night, when she and Mia were settled on their couch eating pizza, Mia finally broached the subject.

"Avery, how's work been going?" She took a large bite of her slice of pizza.

Avery swallowed then took a sip of her soda.

"Fine." She did not want to talk about this tonight. Her emotions were all over the place.

Mia arched her eyebrow. "Just fine?" she asked, disbelieving.

"Yes." That was the trouble with knowing someone as long as she had known Mia. On their first day of kindergarten, a little redheaded boy pushed her down on the playground and Mia had come to her rescue. A blur of blond curls and freckles with the deepest dimples she had ever seen came barreling into the little boy and he didn't even see it coming. Of course, Mia was sent to detention, but Avery had kept her company and they had been inseparable ever since. She hadn't changed much since then. Besides Brady, she was Avery's biggest supporter.

Mia frowned and picked a mushroom off her pizza slice. "Fine, fine or fine, fine?"

"Fine, fine." Avery rolled her eyes and grabbed another piece out of the pizza box on the coffee table, making sure it was from her half with mushrooms and peppers.

"Hmm, I see." Mia set her piece of pizza back on her plate, set the plate on the coffee table, then grabbed Avery's plate and set it beside hers. "Look at me. What's really going on? Don't lie to me. Talk to me." Her puppy dog eyes always did the trick and this time wasn't any different.

Avery rolled her shoulders. "It really is fine. Work has been going surprisingly well. I've enjoyed working on the blog and figuring out what I'm going to write about. Right now, it's once a week but I'm hoping I can get some guest bloggers." She chanced a peek at her pizza and Mia brought her face back around.

"How's Catherine?"

Avery avoided her gaze. "Fine."

"Avery?" Mia growled.

Avery took a deep breath then recounted the last two weeks. "I just need to get my head on straight. By Monday, I need to forge a new game plan. Instead of hoping Catherine will invite me to lunch, I'll bring my own and eat at work. Is it really feasible that someone like her would be interested in me? Mia, I have to be realistic." A relationship with Catherine seemed so out of reach.

"Where is this coming from? You like her, and by what you told me, she at least likes you back. Is it in a romantic sense? I don't know. But, you know what I think. I think you need to go for it. What that is, I don't know, but you need to find out. You at least owe that to yourself."

Avery bit her lip. "What about my job? Is it too soon? What if all this all goes south? What then?"

She shrugged. "I don't know, but you can at least find out. Test the waters."

"How do I do that?" Avery groaned.

She snapped her fingers and jumped up from the couch. "We need a plan of attack. Let's make a list."

"We're not kids anymore." When they were younger, they would have a plan for everything. They had gotten into trouble more than once at school and at home when their plans went off the deep end. As they got older, nothing changed, and their plans seemed to derail so often they gave them up. Mia had to have been serious about everything that was happening to suggest a plan.

"Nonsense. It's been so long, nothing could possibly go wrong." They both stared at each other, then burst out laughing. "Oh hell, I probably just cursed us for life."

"Either way, we'll have a plan, and there are always tacos." Avery reached down and picked Polly up from the floor, where she had been staring at her for the last fifteen minutes. She sat her beside her on the couch and tore up a piece of pizza crust for her.

"Truer words were never spoken." She eyed Polly. "You spoil her too much."

After an hour of constant bickering, they had ten items written on their list. Avery popped the last of her pizza in her mouth and chewed slowly. After she swallowed, she voiced her concerns. "Do you think this will work? It seems so juvenile."

"What? Don't be absurd. What woman doesn't like to be wooed? This," Mia said, holding up the piece of paper, "is our wooing material. Who doesn't like flowers and chocolates? Come on. It's a win-win. Besides, if it doesn't work, at least you would have tried."

Avery drew her knees up to her chest and rested her chin atop them. "I don't think I should sign my name to any gifts. Maybe a poem or something, but not my name. If she reacts badly, I don't want to lose my job over it or the friendship we've been building." She uncurled her legs. She leaned down and pecked Polly on the top of her head. She had been in the trenches with both of them and had come out unscathed every time.

"I agree, actually. This is a good opportunity to up your wooing capabilities." She handed Avery the list. "You can't chicken out now. Avery, I know you. When you get something in your head, you go all in. Don't let this be any different."

"Yes, here's to Operation: Woo." Avery jerked

her head up from the list when there was a knock on her door. "Expecting someone?"

"No." Mia got up and looked through the peephole. "It's Brady." She waited until Avery had folded the list and put it under the couch cushion before undoing the chain lock and opening the door.

"Good evening, ladies."

"Brady," they both said in unison.

Avery accepted the kiss on her cheek and scooted over so he could sit beside her on the couch. "What brings you by?"

He handed them each a candy bar. "You are looking at the new junior editor of my division."

Avery grabbed him and kissed him hard on the cheek. "I knew you could do it."

"I did too." Mia opened her bar and took a big bite.

Avery stopped with the candy bar halfway to her mouth. "Have you guys ever noticed that we use food as a reward for everything that happens to us?"

"Isn't it awesome?" Brady plopped the last of his candy bar in his mouth, then reached for Avery's water to wash it down.

Mia looked at her as if she had grown another head. "Would you really have it any other way? Truthfully, Avery?"

"Well, no, but it was just an observation."

"Keep your negativity to yourself, Avery." He snatched the rest of her candy bar out of her hand and before she could react, stuck it in his mouth.

Just watching them tease each other was such a blessing for her. No matter what, she could always count on them. "I love you guys."

Brady grabbed them each around their shoulders

and pulled them into his sides. "I love you guys, too."

"I ditto that."

Brady tapped her on the shoulder. "I have a couple of hours to kill and wanted to celebrate but didn't want to go out. Grab the remote and pick us something to watch."

After Avery selected Treehouse Masters, she relaxed and stroked Polly's fur. Avery jumped when Mia spoke. "We need a treehouse!"

Brady nodded. "I was just thinking that."

Avery eyed them both. "Where do you purpose we build this treehouse, considering all of us live in an apartment?"

Brady and Mia looked at each other then they both turned slowly toward Avery. "Add it to our bucket list." At this point, their bucket list could probably fill an entire notebook. They would each add things periodically and when any of them achieved something, they would mark it off. So far, they had crossed off hundreds of items.

The last item she had marked off was get a job working in the fashion industry. She knew after tonight Brady would mark off his promotion to junior editor. Mia hadn't marked off anything in a couple of months. Working together, she knew they would mark tons of items off, but there was only one she could mark off for herself. Six years ago, she had added 'get Catherine Davenport to fall in love with her' and she would do her best to fulfill it.

✦✦✦✦

The next morning, Avery left home early, and stopped by a florist close to her apartment building.

She decided on a mixture of different colored lilies. The florist assured her the flowers would be delivered at ten o'clock sharp and confirmed their business was the sole of discretion. She decided not to write on the card herself, but allowed the florist to do it for her.

Her message couldn't be too over the top, so she went with a simple line of text: *My heart beats faster when you're around.* It wasn't a lie, and Catherine had been out of the office so much the last two weeks, the flowers could be from anyone. She thanked the woman and quickly hurried to the coffee shop to pick up her tea and a few black coffees for whoever else might be in the office this early. She usually didn't get to the office until nine, but this morning was an exception. As she handed a coffee to Hannah, she chanced a glance at the clock behind the desk. She was forty minutes early. Hannah thanked her, then went back to her computer.

Avery didn't see another soul until she entered the kitchen, where Catherine stood by the microwave, setting out a few pastries. Every day the pastries were laid out and it had never crossed her mind that Catherine bought them. She smiled at her and set the extra coffees beside the box. Catherine licked her lips, eyed the coffees, then looked back up to Avery. "They're extra. I wasn't sure what everyone would want, so I just got black. You're welcome to one."

"Thank you." At the first sip, Catherine's eyes shut and she moaned. Avery turned away from her, leaned back against the counter, and grabbed up a cheese Danish. "You're here early today?" Catherine did a slow appraisal of Avery from head to toe.

Avery swallowed what was in her mouth, then took a sip of tea to wash it down. "I was up early this morning. I didn't realize how early I was until I looked at the clock behind Hannah's desk. That's not a problem, is it?" Catherine touched her arm and Avery felt the tingles all the way down to her toes.

"No." She smiled. "If you had been twenty minutes earlier you could have eaten breakfast with me."

Avery wasn't sure if that was an invitation but it sure sounded like one and it wouldn't be something she would forget. She would have to make a note to set her alarm thirty minutes earlier every morning. "I'll remember that."

"Please do." She cradled her cup between her hands. "I wanted to ask you—" Her words were cut off when they caught voices coming down the hallway.

"Yes."

Catherine waved her off. "Another time, perhaps."

"Of course." As Camden, Beth, and Sybil walked in, Avery couldn't help but feel that something important had been interrupted. Hopefully, they would get another chance to discuss it. She talked with Sybil for a few minutes then walked to her desk and started working.

At a quarter to ten, she found herself out of the office. The only thing she had wanted to do today was see Catherine's face when the flowers were delivered, but for some unexpected reason her phone had decided today was the day it would die and Catherine had insisted that she go get a new one. After an hour with an incompetent sales person, she walked away with a new phone and back onto the fourteenth floor. Hannah stood up when she stepped off the elevator and Avery stopped in front of the desk. "Yes."

Hannah bit her lip and eyed her up and down,

but didn't say anything. Avery started to feel self-conscious the longer they stood in silence; when the phone rang and Hannah picked it up, she practically ran back down the hallway. The whole episode was weird in a creepy sort of way. She liked Hannah; she hoped she didn't have to reevaluate her judgement of her. She would ask Sybil about her.

Camden asked her how it went and she held up her phone to show everyone. Sybil gave her a thumbs up, then went back to her work, and Beth glared at her. She would win her over; she just had to figure out how.

As soon as she stepped in front of her desk, Catherine called for her. Surely, she didn't know the flowers were from her. Avery shook off her nerves, then turned and walked into the office. She made sure to keep her eyes off the flowers sitting on Catherine's desk. "Is there something I can do for you, Catherine?"

"Please have a seat." Worry crept into the recesses of her mind. Her last evaluation had gone well and traffic to all their media accounts were steadily rising. "Avery, stop worrying. It's nothing bad."

She felt better hearing the words, but her body seemed to have a mind of its own and decided to stay tense. "Good."

Catherine caressed the card beneath her fingertips. "I am quite impressed with what you've done so far. Our Twitter and Instagram followers have nearly doubled and we've had steady traffic to our blog. I know you're in the process of revamping our website, but I was wondering if there is anything else you're working on?"

"Actually, I was hoping to bring this up with you. I think it would be a good idea to have guest bloggers maybe once a week. It will give us an opportunity to feature different people from around the fashion industry. It will potentially drive their followers to us and give them the potential of our followers. We could get established people within the industry and up and comers. Not only designers, but also photographers, models, publishers, etc. There are tons of different avenues we could venture into. We could do a trial run and see how it goes. In exchange for having them guest blog on our page, I will ask them to allow us to guest blog on theirs. A win-win for everyone involved."

Catherine slid her glasses off. "That sounds like a lot of work."

"Not as much as you would think, but there will be a lot involved with it." Avery ran her fingers through her hair. "Right now, I am working on several different blogs for our page for future use. We have several different events coming up; if you're satisfied with my work on the blog so far, I'll put together more articles for those as well." She leaned forward. "I also would like to start taking pictures of your works in progress to post to Instagram."

Before Catherine could speak up, Avery went on. "Not the entire outfit, just maybe a picture of the material, or a section with a button, just something to whet the appetites of the fashion world. And let's face it, if you're involved, everyone who is anybody will be waiting anxiously for the next picture. We can do a one of six photos sort of thing and post one every day. Also, along with revamping your website now, I am also setting up a new website for your ready to wear collections. Not everyone can afford your designer wear, but your new pieces are affordable and nice and I think there should be a divide between the two. I think with the right set-up, we can make a bang when it's time to debut it."

Catherine slipped her glasses back on. "That's an excellent idea." She tapped her fingers on her desk. "I will give you a list of people in the industry that I don't want to be associated with. All I ask for the other ones is that you will let me see the list of potential people and let me okay it first before you agree to allow them to guest blog and vice versa."

"Deal." Avery couldn't wait to get started.

"Good. There is one other thing. I know you will have a lot on your plate, but my daughter, Lincoln's, last day of school is today and she will be coming into the office with me on occasions. I am not asking you to babysit her, but she has seen what you have done with my sites and showed an interest in what you're doing and she wants to get a better read on what occurs here. She has an eye for fashion. Abigail, one the other hand, has decided to take several photography classes, along with joining a bird watchers group; she has also signed up for jewelry making classes. She has a full summer planned. She has shown no interest in fashion, but it's all Lincoln talks about."

Avery knew the twins were fourteen and if getting to know one of her daughters endeared her to Catherine, it was certainly something she would do. "I think it's wonderful you're encouraging them in their hobbies and I have no problem with that. Will she be in tomorrow?" Catherine nodded. "Does she prefer coffee or tea?" At Catherine's raised eyebrow, Avery clarified. "I'll pick her up something to drink. I prefer tea."

"With lemon and honey."

"How'd you know that?" That was certainly unexpected, but just to know Catherine paid attention set her heart racing and she couldn't help the smile that tugged at her lips.

Catherine ran the tip of her glasses over her lips. "Lucky guess."

"Right," Avery drawled. "So?" She had to fight to keep from squirming in her chair. All it took was one look from Catherine to set her on fire.

"Tea."

"And what about you? I know you took the coffee I brought in this morning black, but is that what you prefer?"

"Yes, it is."

"Good to know."

Catherine laid her palms on the desktop. "All right, I guess that's it for now. Keep up the good work."

Avery nodded and her eyes were instantly drawn to the flowers. "Pretty flowers."

Catherine fingered the petals of one of the flowers. "Yes, they are. You were out when they were delivered. Speaking of out. Did you get your phone taken care of?" She slipped her glasses back on and it was the sexiest thing Avery had ever seen.

Avery spent the next ten minutes recounting her horrid experience at the store. Catherine laughed at all the right places, which warmed Avery in places that shouldn't be warmed at work. The sat in silence for a minute until Avery stood up. What she wanted to say was she would see her later; what she said was, "Are you busy for lunch?" She was horrified as soon as the words left her mouth. "It's just...what I meant was..."

"Avery, it's fine. I know what you meant. I know we haven't had lunch together for a few days, but I do have plans today. Another time." She reached for a folder on the corner of her desk.

Avery knew a dismissal when she saw one. "Of course." She wanted to kick herself; instead, she turned and walked toward the door, but stopped and turned around when Catherine spoke again.

"The lilies are beautiful, but my favorite flowers are daisies." Catherine tapped her finger on her lip. "Oh, and Avery, there is always breakfast."

Avery bit her lip, and turned to walk out. "That's good to know."

"If I were you," Catherine said to Avery's back. "I would get all the work done I could today; tomorrow Lincoln will probably talk your ear off."

"Yes, Catherine." As she walked to her desk, she didn't have to turn around to see the smirk on Catherine's face. Tomorrow, she would order lilies again. Even if Catherine did know she sent the flowers, which she might not know, she wouldn't play her trump card and send daisies just yet. That would wait until the time was right. Hopefully, sooner rather than later.

❧❧❧❧

On Friday, Avery had woken up late, and she almost stepped in one of Polly's accidents, before she got her shit together and made it in to work only ten minutes late. Of course, this had to be the day that Camden was in the office early and had berated her the minute she walked in. She didn't think the day would be salvaged. That was until one o'clock rolled around. Catherine stopped by her desk, and told her to grab her purse and follow her. Once they were outside and seated in the backseat of the town car, Avery felt confident enough to ask where they were going.

Catherine turned in her seat to face her. "We are going to my downtown studio. You won't be visiting there much, but I thought now would be just as good of time as any to introduce you to the people that work there. On the rare occasion both of my assistants are absent and I need something delivered to the studio, you may need to do so."

"Okay." She had to temper her excitement or else she would be bouncing in the seat. Being in such close quarters with Catherine was torture, especially when Avery would get a whiff of Catherine's signature perfume. It was a combination of sweet and spicy and wreaked havoc on Avery's nerves. Not to mention when Catherine had walked into work that morning Avery had about fell out of her chair. She had paired a pair of cream-colored trousers with a long sleeve white button up top and the black vest she wore over top of it hugged her curves to perfection. Not to mention the insane amount of cleavage that was on display.

Catherine spoke without looking up from her phone. "After I finish up my business with the studio, we can grab a late lunch if you want to?"

"I would really like that." Avery relaxed back in the seat, content just to sit quietly with the other woman. The studio was small, but, like Catherine's office, was modern, and sleek. After introductions, Avery wandered around and her eye caught on a fantastic black dress hanging in the corner. She was about to ask about it when Catherine touched her arm and informed her if they wanted something to eat they would need to leave. With one last look to the dress, Avery followed her out of the building.

They were only at the studio for thirty minutes, but it had seemed far longer. Once they were seated, and their drinks were delivered, Avery asked a question she had been wondering about. "Why fashion?" She had never read a direct answer in any of the interviews Catherine had given.

Catherine took a sip of her water before answering. "I have always loved to create. And to have my designs draping a woman's body is a dream come true. There are so many different fabrics, and to find a way to make them pleasing and to make sure they fall correctly is challenging at times, but I love it. What I am surprised about is the interest that people still take in my designs. The fashion industry is very competitive, and for me to still be at the top, at my age, and after being in the business for so many years, is astounding. Now your turn. Why fashion?"

"I see clothing as wearable art. Even the lines of a simple pencil skirt can be a game changer. Fashion allows everyone to have an even playing field. There is something for everyone. People have their favorites, but doesn't everyone? Fashion allows you to make a statement no matter what you're wearing. Be it a good one, or a bad one."

Catherine waited until their salads had been delivered to speak. "I want my girls to be who they want to be, but I felt a bit relieved when Lincoln took an interest in fashion. Abigail on the other hand, who knows. If they're happy, I'm not too worried."

"My dad wanted me to be a lawyer, but I had no interest. My mom's only wish was for me to graduate college. She doesn't care what I do, if I enjoy it." In fact, it had caused a massive fight with her biological dad when she didn't go to law school, but she needn't had worried about his approval, because it was only a month later that she decided to come out to her family, and he cut ties with her.

"Do you have any interest in designing?"

Avery pushed her lettuce around her plate with her fork. "No. I will leave that to the experts. I enjoy wearing fashion, not creating it." Avery pushed her plate to the side. "What I have been enjoying is writing for the blog, more than I thought I would. I have been doing a bit of research on freelance work and might try my hand at different articles and see if I can't get them published."

"If you want, I can look at them after you're finished. No guarantees, but I will see what some of my friends in the publishing industry think of them. It is a competitive field, but what I've seen so far from you is very promising."

Avery kept her shock at bay and was at a loss for words when Catherine tapped her on the hand bringing her back to reality. "That would be fantastic." She stumbled over the words. "I don't know what to say." The offer was certainly unexpected, especially considering how busy Catherine had been lately.

"Then don't say anything. I don't mind. Just don't spread it around the office." She winked and took a sip of her water.

"I won't." Avery took another sip of water. "Would it be possible for me to buy the dress I saw at your studio?"

Catherine smiled. "The black one? With the gold stitching?"

"Yes. It was spectacular."

Catherine laughed. "I'll see what I can do. For such a simple dress, it took me almost three weeks to design." She waved her hand in the air. "It just wouldn't come to me. Some come far easier than others."

"Do you ever get so far along in the process, then you go blank, and scrap the entire thing?"

"No. I keep every sketch I've ever attempted. You never know when inspiration will hit. The other day I was looking through one of my earlier sketch books and was amazed at how far I've come."

Avery tried not to look too excited. "I would love to see them and if you would permit me, I could post an early sketch of yours once a week on your social media accounts."

Catherine tilted her head. "I don't mind you looking at them, but I would rather not have them posted. They're personal."

"Done." Even that Catherine would allow her to see them felt like a hurdle jumped. "I would love to see them."

"I'll see what I can do. I know Lincoln and Abigail both love looking at them. I think that if you're serious about your craft, you will keep learning and growing. I will never stop challenging myself to do better. If that time would ever come, I would hang up my needle."

"I can't see yourself ever phoning it in and I haven't known you that long. When I saw you a few years ago, I believe you were just as excited to teach as I was to learn."

"When was this?"

Avery blushed and fiddled with the tablecloth. "About six years."

Catherine tapped her finger on her lips. "Accessories through the years."

"Yes. I learned so much that day. I sat through every presentation, but yours by far blew me away."

"You already have the job, Avery." She winked. "There's no need to suck up."

Avery grinned and bit her lip. "Well, since I'm sucking up, please allow me to say you look fantastic today."

Catherine's hand that was twirling her straw in her glass stilled and Avery could have sworn she saw a pink tint brushing Catherine's checks. "Charmer."

Avery laughed. "Well, when you have it, you have it."

"And I guess you have it?"

"You have no idea."

"Oh, I believe I have an idea, but that's neither here nor there and I believe it's time to get back to work."

"Thank you for lunch. You'll have to allow me to return the favor."

"I'll remember that." After the check was delivered, Catherine paid the bill, and they headed back to the office. It was a pleasant lunch, but it was still an opportunity to get to know a bit more about what made Catherine tick. The flirting didn't hurt either.

The ride back to the office was quiet, but not uncomfortable. As soon as they entered the building, Catherine nodded at the security guards, who waved them through, then they headed for the elevators. Avery smiled at Catherine when the elevator doors shut behind her, then quickly stepped into the next one when it became available. Today was a good day; hopefully tomorrow would even better.

※ ※ ※ ※

Monday flew by and still no sign of Lincoln, but on Thursday, when Avery entered the small kitchen area at seven-thirty sharp, Catherine was standing beside the counter with a young woman by her side. Lincoln was almost as tall as her mother and had the same blue eyes. Her long red hair fell past her shoulders and was cut in varying lengths. Although her mother was one of the leading fashion designers in the world, Lincoln wore a pair of faded Levi's and a University of Tennessee T-shirt. "Good morning."

"Lincoln," Catherine said. "This is Avery. Avery, Lincoln."

They shook hands and Avery bit her lip as Lincoln took in her outfit. It was the first time she had worn a C.D. Design since she started and Mia had insisted she should wear the black sheath dress. She had paired it with a red belt and a pair of four-inch Prada heels. From the looks Catherine threw her way, at least one of them appreciated her outfit and Avery had to fight the urge not to make a fool of herself in front of them. The last thing she wanted was to make a bad first impression with Lincoln.

Lincoln rolled her eyes and picked up a donut. "You know wearing her clothes won't get you in her good graces." She eyed Avery, then the donut, before putting it back in the box and wiping her hands on a napkin.

"Lincoln," Catherine said in warning. Avery didn't know if it was because of what she said or because she put the donut back in the box.

Instead of asking for clarification, Avery picked up a cup and handed it to Lincoln, who was a miniature version of Catherine and Avery couldn't help but like her even with her snarky attitude. "It's actually the first time, since I've worked here, that I've worn one of your mother's designs. Here, take it. It's tea."

With a bit of reluctance, Lincoln accepted the tea and took a tentative sip. "Thank you."

Well, at least she had manners. "You're welcome." She handed another cup to Catherine and placed the rest on the desk beside the donuts.

Catherine picked up three food containers off the counter. "Ladies, we'll eat in my office." Catherine led the way and Avery hung back with Lincoln. She wanted to make sure the young woman didn't feel left out. This would be the third day eating breakfast with Catherine and she couldn't wait to see what she had brought for them today.

Avery pushed her and Lincoln's chairs closer to the desk and sat down. Lincoln flopped down in hers and set her cup beside Avery's on the desk. Avery accepted the container and opened it. A large fluffy vegetable and bacon omelet lay nestled inside. It smelled heavenly. "Thank you."

Catherine grinned. "You're welcome."

After Lincoln's first bite, she turned to her mother. "No crab meat?"

Avery cringed, and stopped with her first bite to her lips. "No," Catherine said and Avery instantly felt guilty. Just because she couldn't have it, didn't mean that they should deprive themselves of it, but before she could protest, Catherine spoke up again. "If we eat with Avery, we will not be eating seafood. She is deathly allergic." Lincoln turned toward her, but the contempt she expected to see on her face never came. Instead, she looked surprised and shocked. She glanced between Avery and her mother, smirked, then took another bite of her food.

What was that look about? "You don't have to deprive yourselves on my account. Really."

Lincoln snorted. "Don't waste your breath. When Mom gets something in her head, nobody can change it." She slowly turned toward Avery, took a bite of her food, and chewed it, but she never looked away.

What did that mean? Lincoln obviously knew something she didn't. But what? Surely she couldn't already tell how she felt about her mother. That would be awkward. Even more awkward than it was right now. After finishing half of her omelet, she finally looked up to catch Catherine looking at her. Without breaking eye contact, Catherine tilted her head and bit her lip. It was the most endearing thing Avery had ever seen before and she couldn't decipher the look in the other woman's eyes. It was the first time she had seen that look directed at her. It held warmth, caring, and something she couldn't decipher. The moment was broken when a hand started waving itself between them.

Lincoln snapped her fingers. "This food is too good to waste."

Everyone finished their food in relative silence and by the time Avery threw the empty containers away, the first employees had started to trickle in. As soon as she sat down at her desk, another chair found itself beside hers and Lincoln sat down next to her.

"So," Lincoln said. "Breakfast was good. Don't you think so?"

"It was." She figured it was best to keep her answers to a minimum. Lincoln would probably read something into everything she said. Best not to give her any ideas.

"Mom's been getting flowers every day this week." She fiddled with the paper clips in the container on Avery's desk.

Avery fought with herself not to rip the paper clips from Lincoln's fingers. "Yes."

"She has really enjoyed getting them." Lincoln dropped the paper clips, one at a time, back into the box. She then turned toward Avery with a knowing look on her face and Avery fought the flush that was creeping up her neck.

She would not show her hand to this teenager. "It seemed so."

"Do you know anything about that?" She tapped her finger on her lips just like her mother. Where it sent shivers down her spine when Catherine did it, Lincoln just annoyed her.

"No."

"You seem like a nice person. So, I'll tell it to you straight. My mom doesn't have the best track record with women. Most of the time they see her as unreachable and untouchable. She is neither. Just because she wears certain types of clothes or acts in a certain way doesn't mean she is cold or indifferent to anyone around her. I believe you should act a certain way when you're the boss. Don't confuse her work persona with her home one, but what I've seen so far, you haven't encountered the work persona yet." She tapped her finger on her lips again. "I wonder why that is?" Her eyes got wide. "Do you have any idea?" She pointed her finger at Avery.

Avery leaned close to her. "Cut the crap, kid. What do you want?"

Lincoln moved in close until they were almost nose-to-nose. "I want to know what your intentions are toward my mother."

Avery drew back quickly to put distance between them. "What? I work for her. She's my boss." Avery stuttered, then turned away from her and fired up her laptop, but she could feel Lincoln's penetrating gaze on her.

"Well, if that's the way you act toward her, I won't have to worry about your intentions because you won't have any. The flowers are a nice touch, but you need to up your game. She loves chocolate and none of that fancy crap. She likes the miniature Hershey chocolate bars and Kit-Kats." Lincoln rested her elbows on the desk next to Avery's arm and leaned into her space. "Do you know that sometimes all we hear at dinner is Avery this and Avery that?"

Avery whipped her head around. "Really?" she asked eagerly and regretted the word as soon as it slid off her tongue.

Lincoln grinned. "Gotcha."

Avery closed her eyes, then opened them and focused on the spreadsheet currently occupying her laptop's screen. She couldn't believe she had let this kid play her. But, if Lincoln already knew, it wouldn't hurt to have her help. "Does she really like those chocolates or were you lying?"

Lincoln had abandoned the paperclips and was focusing on her phone. "She really likes them."

"Were you serious about her talking about me?"

"Let me ask you something first?"

"Okay."

"Are you really interested in my mother? Because where I'm sitting there is a huge age difference between you two."

Avery scrunched her nose up. "Not as big as you might think. Only twenty or so years."

"That's a pretty big difference. If you just have a crush, end it now. But," she held her hand up. "If you have feelings for her, real feelings, you need to up your game. Step up to the plate. My mother is amazing and she deserves to be wooed. Everyone expects, because she has a lot of money, that she should be the one doing the wooing, but she deserves better than that. Are you better than that, Avery?" Avery cringed at the words. Woo her. She thought that was what she was doing. Obviously not and yes, Lincoln was right; Catherine did deserve that. "The flowers were an excellent start but you need to do more, and for the record, her favorite flower is the daisy."

Avery nodded. "I know, she told me after the first flower delivery."

Lincoln looked astonished. "So, why is she still getting lilies delivered?" She snapped her fingers.

"I didn't want her to know they were from me in case she hated them."

"What? Wait a minute. What did you say after she said that daisies were her favorite?"

"I told her I would remember that."

"What are you waiting for? A gold-plated invitation? A marching band? Even Abby and I have more sense than you."

"I..." What was she waiting for? "I don't know. I just..." She sighed. She turned her chair fully toward Lincoln. "I wanted to be sure she liked me too. Not just like liked, but like liked. I like this job, so I wanted to be sure. Right now, it feels like we're becoming friends and—"

"Stop. Has it ever dawned on you that, I don't know, maybe if you send her favorite flowers, things might progress to the next level and she might see your true intentions? I can see why you haven't asked her out on a proper date yet, because of your job and you don't want to ruin that. I get that, but if you are going to continue to send her flowers, why not make it her favorite? You are going to continue to send her flowers, right?"

Avery ran her fingers through her hair. "I thought next week I would have chocolate delivered instead. Maybe a few other things as well." Maybe this wooing business wasn't such a good idea after all.

"If you have the money, send both. Trust me. She will love it." Lincoln nodded as if it was the greatest idea in the world.

"I know you're her daughter, but how do you know that she like likes me? Maybe she just wants to be friends."

Lincoln fiddled with the stapler, before Avery took it away from her. "I have one word for you; shellfish." She held up one finger.

Not back to the shellfish thing again. "What does that mean?" She opened her drawer put her stapler inside, along with her Tenth Doctor pop figure and a few other trinkets that she didn't want Lincoln to get her hands on. Before shutting the drawer, she took the small container of paperclips and dumped them in as well.

Lincoln picked up a pen and tapped it on the edge of the desk. "My mother loves shellfish. For her to think of you before that is huge. She has never given that type of consideration to anyone she has ever dated before."

She supposed that was a good thing. "Has anyone she every dated been deathly allergic to it before?"

"No, but she has never given up something she loved so much for someone else. Well, except for me." At Avery's questioning look, Lincoln explained. "I asked her to stop using, buying, and wearing real fur, and she agreed. Oh, and Abby asked her to stop eating veal and she agreed."

"That's interesting." There was a lot she still didn't know about her. Avery bit her lip and leaned back in her chair. Of their own accord, her eyes strayed to Catherine's office, whose gaze lingered on them. Lincoln slipped her arm around Avery's shoulders, pulled her close, and waved at her mom with a cheeky grin on her face. Catherine rolled her eyes, but waved back.

"See," Lincoln said and moved her arm, focusing all her attention on Avery again. "She likes you. Now we should make a list." Avery rolled her eyes, but opened her purse and took out a folded piece of paper. She handed it to Lincoln, who proceeded to open it and nodded. "I'm glad to see you've thought about this. Now, let's add to it and for goodness sake, you can send her more than one thing at a time. Go big or go home. Amateurs," she muttered.

After Lincoln added one last time, Avery accepted the paper back and looked it over. There wasn't anything to object about but some of the items seemed a bit personal. Like her favorite type of scented candle. Catherine didn't burn candles in the office. "But, if I send her the scented candle she will probably know you told me."

Lincoln nodded. "It's a good plan. That way she will know I approve."

"You do?"

"You're not so bad and to answer your question from earlier, she does talk about you a lot. I'll talk to Abby tonight and explain the situation." Lincoln pulled Avery's laptop toward her and scanned the document.

Avery had to admit, she had felt a certain vibe from Catherine, and she had been staring at her a lot more, but was it enough to put her heart on the line? She wasn't a hundred percent sure, but if she let this chance pass through her fingertips, she would never forgive herself and would regret not going for it. Here was her best friend and Catherine's daughter telling her to take a chance. She shook her head. *Go big, or go home.* "So, where can I buy this candle?"

❧❧❧❧

The next day dawned bright and early. Too early in Avery's opinion. She had done exactly what Lincoln had suggested. After leaving work the previous night, she had stopped to buy the candle Catherine preferred, along with a small bag of miniature Hershey chocolate bars and a white chocolate Kit-Kat. She had the items nestled in a small basket and entered the florist shop. She set her package down on the counter when Sheila smiled at her and walked in from the back room. She had been in so many times in the past week and a half, they were practically friends.

"Avery, good morning. Same as always?"

Avery shook her head. "No. Today I would like a bouquet of daisies." She trumped down her nerves and decided to go for it.

She smiled and nodded. "I have a nice assortment of Gerbera daisies." She walked into the back room and returned quickly with a nice collection of pink, red, peach, and purple flowers. "Something like this?"

"Yes." They were beautiful. No wonder they were Catherine's favorite.

"Would you like the same size as usual? These

are a bit cheaper than the lilies."

"Just make them as big for the price I usually pay. Also." She pushed the package toward her. "Can you include this in your delivery?"

"Of course." She in turn handed Avery a small, blank card. "This delivery feels different. Do you want to write on the card yourself?"

Avery accepted the card and bit her lip. What to write? After a few minutes, she had the perfect idea and neatly wrote on the card, before giving it back. Sheila smirked, but didn't say anything, then showed her the bouquet. "It's really nice. Thank you." She tried to disguise her handwriting, but didn't know if she had succeeded.

"You're welcome."

She had texted Lincoln before she left home to tell her she wouldn't be able to have breakfast with them, so when she walked into work, surprised filtered across her face at seeing Lincoln already seated at her desk and a food container in front of her laptop.

Lincoln looked up from her phone and nodded at her. Today she wore a navy skirt and a sleeveless, cream V-neck blouse, paired with a stylish pair of sandals. Avery had to admit she looked very grown up, but she still held a bit of mischief in her eyes. Lincoln pointed to the container. "Mom insisted. It's crepes with diced fruit. I just took it out of the fridge for you."

Avery swallowed the lump in her throat and focused on the takeout container. She knew she had made the right decision with her delivery for today. Lincoln rolled her eyes and told her to eat, but she shook her head and walked toward Catherine's office. She sat behind her desk and was looking out the window. Avery admired her profile for a few moments, before knocking on the door. Catherine slowly turned to her and smiled at her before motioning for her to come in. "Thank you for breakfast. I had to take care of something this morning or I would have been here."

Catherine waved her words off. "No need to explain yourself. Eggs wouldn't have kept so I got you something different. I hope you like it."

"I'm sure I will. No doubt about that."

"Well," Catherine tapped her pencil on the desk. "That's good to know." Avery couldn't help but admire her long neck that was adorned with a simple gold chain. She traced the lines of Catherine's neck with her eyes. Avery licked her lips and Catherine's eyes darkened. Avery stepped away from the wall and steadied her breathing.

Avery pointed behind her. "I...should eat."

"Yes." Catherine's voice was softer than normal. "You should."

"Okay. Okay." She backed away from the desk. "I am sure I will talk to you later." She ran her hands down the sides of her pants legs.

Catherine winked at her then slipped her glasses on. "I'm sure you will."

Fighting the urge to run up to her and wrap her arms around her, Avery high-tailed it back to her desk, ignoring the smirk on Lincoln's face, and started to eat her breakfast.

When she was finished eating, she and Lincoln got started on their list for the day. While she updated their sites, and worked on the new website, Lincoln read over her articles for the blogs and complied a bigger list of guest bloggers they wanted to contact. She would randomly check their list against Catherine's to make sure no one overlapped. The last thing they wanted was to give Catherine back a sub-par list.

They were both so caught up in their work, they didn't notice the deliveryman arrive and walk into Catherine's office. It wasn't until Sybil walked over to them that they realized something was up. Avery's eyes were glued to the office and without a word, Lincoln stood up and walked toward her mother.

"I wonder who has been sending her the flowers?" Sybil asked, then tapped Avery on the shoulder, and walked back to her desk.

After the deliveryman left, Catherine and Lincoln stood side-by-side with their backs to her. When Lincoln slipped her arm around her mom's waist, Avery started to get a bad feeling, so she sat back down and concentrated on what she was working on before the distraction. What had she been thinking? Go big or go home. What a crock. She ran her fingers through her hair, and dared a glance up. They were both looking at her with unreadable expressions on their faces. Avery swallowed. What was she supposed to do? She had never been good at this type of thing before. Why had she listened to Mia and Lincoln? One was a kid and the other one hadn't had a date in the last six months.

"Avery." She whipped her head around when Camden called her name. Thankful for the reprieve, even though they hadn't warmed up to each other yet, she stood quickly and practically ran across the room to join him. "Catherine said you wanted pictures of her works in progress."

"Yes." She pulled out her phone and took several discreet shots of numerous parts of the skirt and blouse. After Camden approved them, he touched her on the arm.

"Are you okay?" The sympathetic look on his face put Avery on edge.

"Of course."

"Look, I know it's not my place, but I can see the way you look at her. It's just, this must be hard on you."

"Pardon?" There was no way Camden could possibly know. What was he playing at?

"The flowers and the delivery today. Whomever she is seeing it must be getting serious if they sent daisies. They're her favorite and not many people know that."

Oh. Avery sucked in a breath. Okay. Camden didn't know she had been sending the flowers, but he did know Avery had a crush. She didn't know if she should feel offended that Camden didn't even consider that she sent the flowers or not. Avery smiled but it didn't reach her eyes. "It is what it is."

Camden didn't look convinced. "If you're sure."

She frowned. "I am and I should get back and work on our campaign for these photos."

"Of course. I'm here if you need to talk or anything. You have been doing a good job and I wouldn't want anything to interfere with that. You wouldn't be the first person to get a crush on the boss."

"All good." She left before she would say something she would regret later. So, Camden wasn't looking out for her at all, he was looking out for the job. When she reached her desk, Lincoln was already seated and an open Hershey package lay on the table. So did Lincoln like the Hershey bars, not Catherine? Great. Just great. Avery didn't bother looking at her; instead, she uploaded the pictures and started working on them. After an hour, Lincoln slid a Hershey bar toward her and Avery cut her eyes in her direction.

Lincoln frowned at her. "What's wrong with you? Your big delivery went off without a hitch."

She waved of her words. "Nothing."

"You're pouting. Let me tell you. That's real attractive."

Avery ran her hand down her face, leaned back in her chair, crossed her arms across her chest, and regarded the person sitting next to her. Lincoln was typing and didn't bother to look in her direction. She didn't dare look toward Catherine's office, afraid of what she would see on her face. Disgust, indifference, or pity. Catherine had to know that the flowers had been from her, especially now. What did she think?

Without looking away from her laptop, Lincoln spoke. "Why did you write that on the card?"

Avery leaned her head back and counted the tiles on the ceiling. When she had her anxiety pushed back to a manageable level, she looked back at the young woman who was looking back at her. "Was there something wrong with it?"

"That's not what I asked."

She didn't owe this kid anything, but her eyes were just like her mother's; it was hard to ignore her. "I meant it. I don't know what else you want me to say."

"It was." Lincoln threw her pencil down. "It was a bit reckless. I didn't know you had it in you. Did you really think that would get you closer to getting in my mom's pants?"

"What?" Who the hell did she think she was? "Now wait a minute." The longer they sat staring at each other, the more her anger started to boil and her anxiety started to surface. She had to get out of here. Her eyes darted around the office, before coming full circle and stopping at a smirking Lincoln.

"It was over the top, and pretty cheesy. I mean, come on, who says something like that?"

Avery wanted to smack that smirk off her face. She took a deep breath, but her heart continued to race. She slammed her laptop shut, threw it into her bag along with several folders that were piled on her desk, and turned back to Lincoln, whose smirk had vanished. "I'm going home. I don't care what you tell anybody. I can't stay here."

"Wait." Lincoln grabbed her arm. She looked scared and kept stealing glances at her mother's office. "I was just teasing. I needed to know how you felt. I am only trying to protect Mom. Please."

"Sure you were. It's always nice to be made fun of, isn't it? To laugh when someone lays their heart on the line. Go big or go home." She leaned closer to her. "I'll work with you here, but that's all. I knew I shouldn't have listened to you." If that's what Lincoln thought, then what did Catherine think?

"It's not like that," Lincoln pleaded and reached for her arm.

"Lincoln," Catherine called from her office.

She threw her arm off. "You should go. Your mother is calling you."

"What do I tell her?" She stood up with her hands on her hips.

"I don't care."

"Seriously, you're acting like a kid, Avery."

Avery jumped away from her, ignored everyone when they called her name, and walked past Hannah and into the elevator. She didn't want to deal with any of this right now. She'd already made a fool of herself once; that was enough for today.

As she stepped out of the elevator, her phone rang. Catherine's number flashed back at her. Taunting her. She hit ignore and turned her phone on silence before she slipped it into her pocket and started walking toward home. How could she have been so stupid? They hadn't even gone on a date yet. Who in their right mind writes, *to know you is to love you,* to a woman she isn't even dating?

The next morning, Avery groaned and rolled over in bed, only to come face to face with Polly. Avery laughed when Polly licked her nose and started dancing around her. Even with a heavy heart, she jumped out of bed and headed into the living room with Polly hot on her heels, where she came to an abrupt stop.

She had completely forgotten it was Saturday and what today was. Every three or four months her and her friends had a Harry Potter themed weekend. The host house decorated and provided snacks. Today was she and Mia's turn. The living room was decorated like the Gryffindor common room.

"Glad to see you're up," Mia said from the kitchen, where she was assembling treat boxes for everyone. There were already trays of snacks lining the counter top.

"Let me take Polly out and get dressed then I'll help you."

"Make it quick."

After a short walk and a relaxing shower, she dressed in a Slytherin Quidditch outfit. She slipped a small shirt decorated with all the houses on it onto Polly's quivering little body and they both walked into the living room, where Mia was talking to someone on the phone. Her phone. Avery narrowed her eyes when Mia handed her the phone.

"That was your boss."

Avery looked panicked. "Why did you answer?"

She threw her hands up. "Why didn't you? She sounded worried. She tried calling you yesterday. Something about missing sketches. She was wondering if you had brought them home. If you have them, she would like you to take them to her house."

"What?" Avery walked back to the corner of the room, where she had dumped her bag the day before. Sure enough, there was a red folder inside with dozens of sketches inside. They all had Catherine's signature in the bottom right hand corner. Lincoln must have laid it on the desk yesterday and she had grabbed it in her haste to flee by mistake. What the hell had she been thinking yesterday? She slumped against the wall as reality set in. What had she done?

Mia rolled her eyes and kicked her foot. "Also, Lincoln has been texting you."

Avery groaned and scrolled through the texts. In every one, she apologized. Avery closed her eyes when she read the last text:

I am so sorry. I really didn't mean it. Please, Avery, Mom is really worried. You just left. I really do like you and so does Mom. I am sure Abby will when she meets you. She really liked the flowers and the other gifts. Don't do this. Yes, the card was a lot to take in. Be honest; you would think so too. I just needed to know you were sincere. I really am sorry.

Avery stood and pushed away from the wall with the folder clutched in her hand. "Shit." How had her life veered so off course? "I don't even know her address." Mia took a piece of paper off the counter and handed it to her. "I have to help you finish decorating."

"I can handle that. Avery, she seemed really upset."

"The folder is safe. I'll take it to her now."

Mia smacked her in the head. "You're being stupid. I think the folder was just an excuse. She was upset you just left work. I know what happened. I talked to Lincoln. She really is sorry and you have to realize she is just a kid."

"I know. But when she started making fun of me, I felt all my fears coming back full force and could feel the beginning of a panic attack. I had to get out of there."

"You didn't even get Catherine's reaction to the flowers."

"No, that had been the last thing on my mind after what transpired with Lincoln."

"Don't worry about Lincoln; we had a very enlightening talk. She knows about your panic attacks and will tread lightly. I even put in a few good words for you."

"Thank you." The last thing she wanted to do was see Catherine this morning, but she would take the folder to her house. She eyed her outfit, then Polly's, and shrugged. It wouldn't be the first time a grown woman and her dog, dressed in Harry Potter costumes, walked down the streets in New York. She squared her shoulders, shared a silent conversation with Polly, then nodded. Polly barked. Mia rolled her eyes.

Lincoln was right; she did act like a kid yesterday. She let her insecurities get the best of her and could have possibly ruined everything. It was time to start acting like an acceptable partner for Catherine. She may have gone a bit too far with the last card, but it was the truth. Now she just needed to show her in her actions. She may not feel comfortable asking her out yet, but she could do numerous other things for her. Flowers and chocolates were nice, but she always seemed stressed at the office, even with her two assistants. On Monday, Avery would consider ways of easing the pressure Catherine put on herself.

Today, she would deliver the folder, apologize for leaving, and act as if nothing weird had happened the day before. She wouldn't pretend the flowers were never delivered, but she wouldn't bring it up either.

"You leaving?" Mia called to her.

"I'll be back as soon as possible." She rummaged in the drawer by the door and pulled out a Harry Potter leash, then proceeded to clip it onto Polly's owl splattered collar.

"Good luck."

"We don't need luck." Mia's laugh followed them out the door and into the elevator. They received quite a few stares as they walked down the busy sidewalk, but Avery paid them no attention. It took them a little over thirty minutes to reach Catherine's townhouse. She and Polly exchanged looks. "I know, Polly, what have we gotten ourselves into?" Before she could chicken out, Avery rang the doorbell.

Her heart sped up when the door opened to reveal Catherine in a pair of black trousers, and an off the shoulder, pale blue sweater. It was the first time she had ever seen her look so casual and to top it off, she was barefoot. Avery had to remind herself to breathe. Her feet were rooted to the spot as she looked up at Catherine. She fought the urge to run her fingers through her hair.

Catherine did a slow appraisal of her from head to toe. "I wasn't aware there was a costume convention in town this weekend." Avery could tell she tried to hide her smile, but she failed.

Avery stood firm, but couldn't help the blush that covered her neck and face. Damn her pale complexation "Oh, well…"

"Wow," Lincoln said from behind Catherine. "That is awesome, and look at the dog."

"Polly."

Lincoln came closer to her. "What?"

"Lincoln, stand back and allow Avery and her dog inside."

"Her name is Polly." Before she could say hello to Catherine, Lincoln threw her arms around her and hugged her. Catherine looked surprised and Avery masked her surprise and quickly pushed her away, ignoring the flicker of pain that crossed Lincoln's face before Avery knelt next to Polly. "Stop growling. These are our friends." She tapped the dog on the nose. "They're friends." She waved Lincoln over and she knelt next to them. "This is Lincoln." Polly growled again, but a stern look from Avery and she stopped. She looked at Lincoln's face. "I wasn't pushing you away."

"I know now. It's all right. I really am sorry," she said quietly.

"I overreacted yesterday. Let's put it down to a lapse in judgment on both our parts."

Lincoln grinned. "Deal."

Avery looked up as another person joined them. She was a carbon copy of Lincoln, expect for her haircut; Abigail's was cut in a bob. Avery held out her hand, but Abigail ignored it. Unlike her sister, Abigail seemed to be the least friendly of the two. "Abigail, it's nice to meet you." Abigail assessed her then turned and walked out of the room.

"Don't mind her," Lincoln said. "She's being a butt."

Avery chuckled. "Okay."

"Lincoln, language."

"Sorry, Mom." She looked sheepish.

"Polly, be good." They both stood up and Avery slipped the bag off her shoulder and lifted the folder out, handing it to Catherine. "I'm sorry about rushing out yesterday."

"Don't worry about it. We all have an off day." She clutched the folder to her chest. "You're okay now?"

"Yes." Well, as good as she could be, standing in Catherine's living room, so close to the object of her desire. She instantly felt at ease, knowing Catherine didn't hold anything she done the previous day against her.

"Good." Catherine glanced at Polly. "Introduce me."

Avery picked Polly up and held her under her arm. Polly sniffed Catherine's outstretched fingers then licked them. Avery gasped. "She likes you. She usually doesn't take to anyone that quickly."

"So I shouldn't be offended?" Lincoln asked in mock outrage.

"No. She can be a bit territorial. She still doesn't like my parents and she only tolerates Mia." She kissed Polly on the head. "Polly, this is Catherine." Catherine rubbed under her chin and Polly went limp in Avery's arms. Avery huffed. "Traitor."

"So," Lincoln said. "Why are you so dressed up?"

Abigail came back into the hallway and stood next to her sister, eyeing both her and Polly as if she was trying to figure them out.

Avery had the good grace to blush, but wouldn't be embarrassed by their weekend plans. It was a tradition. "Every few months, my friends and I have a Harry Potter themed weekend. It was Mia's and my weekend to host. We decorate and provide themed treats. I ordered tons of stuff and Mia is putting the finishing touches on the living room. We tossed a coin and since she was sorted into Gryffindor, the living room is decorated like their common room. That's all right, Polly and I are proud to be Slytherins."

Lincoln smiled. "That's awesome. Like chocolate frogs and stuff."

Avery ran her fingers through her hair. "I may have gotten carried away with the treats, but we only host every few months. So," she shrugged. "I splurged."

"We have a weekend a few times a year that we watch all the movies back-to-back."

"Really? What houses are you both in?" Lincoln puffed out her chest and Avery didn't even have to ask. She turned to Catherine. "And I know what house you're in." That was such a turn on.

Catherine huffed. "So you do."

"Really, Mom? You told her what house you're in?" Abigail asked, in disbelief.

"I did."

"Hmm." Abigail still looked unconvinced.

"Are you also in Gryffindor?" Avery asked her.

When it didn't look like she was going to answer, Lincoln squeezed her hand. "Yes." Avery got the feeling Abigail didn't like her; she would have to get to the bottom of it. She got a bad feeling when Abigail grinned at her. "The last person that walked out on Mom at the office was fired."

Avery whipped her head around toward Catherine. "Catherine, I'm sorry."

Catherine addressed Abigail. "I am not going to fire Avery." When Abigail opened her mouth to speak, Catherine held up her hand. "It is not up for discussion, Abigail."

"Whatever."

Avery had a feeling she would have her work cut out for her winning Abigail over, if the looks she was throwing her way was any indication. "So, I should probably be going. I promised Mia I would help her finish and it's almost eleven. The first movie will start at twelve."

"So soon?" Catherine asked

Avery wanted to stay, but they had been planning this weekend for months and Mia would kill her. "Yes."

"Thank you for bringing the sketches over so quickly."

"We could come," Lincoln blurted out.

"Lincoln, it's rude to invite yourself to someone else's party," Catherine chastised.

"Sorry." She didn't look sorry, and she and Abigail seemed to share a silent conversation.

Avery grinned and didn't see a reason why they couldn't attend. There would be plenty of food and treats. She pulled her phone out, sent a quick text to Mia, and received a reply just as quickly. She caught sight of Abigail out of the corner of her eye, who, for the first time, seemed to be interested in her. "All three of you are welcome to join our party. Besides me and Mia, there will be four other people." Catherine still looked uncertain. Maybe she'd overstepped again. "Or not."

"Mom, can we? We weren't doing anything anyway." Abigail spoke up.

Catherine sighed, before turning to Avery. "How long will this party run for?"

"Oh." Avery scratched her cheek. "Until tomorrow when we finish the films. We also play Harry themed board games. All of us usually camp out in the living room, but you're welcome to use my bed." She almost stopped herself from blushing, but failed when she saw the mischief in Catherine's eyes.

"Your bed, really, Avery?"

"Like I said. We make a weekend of it and I'll be sleeping in the living room anyway." She shrugged and turned her attention to the girls.

Lincoln bounced on her heels. "That's even better. Mom, we will have so much fun."

"But," Avery said. "It is a theme weekend." She pointed to her and Polly's outfits. "You have to dress appropriately. Or if you have a costume, you can wear that as well. You'd be surprised how far some of us would go to look authentic."

Catherine took a step in her direction even as Lincoln and Abigail ran up the stairs before she even agreed. "Are you sure it's okay for us to join you?"

"Of course." Avery fought to keep her two feet on the ground, but inside she was jumping for joy. Having Catherine at her home for two days was a dream come true and a nightmare all rolled into one. Thank goodness Mia was the only one who knew about her crush. She didn't think she could handle it if Catherine found out about her feelings this weekend. Although, she was pretty sure Catherine already knew she had a crush on her. Avery inhaled and Catherine's perfume drifted her way. It was custom made for her, but Avery knew that even if someone else wore it, they would never smell as good as Catherine did. And it wasn't a fragrance she would be forgetting anytime soon.

"Will there be alcohol?"

Avery glanced at Catherine's lips then quickly away. "No. We keep it clean. Our first weekend we threw the party, alcohol was served and it was a disaster. We banned it ever since."

Catherine grasped Avery's forearm. "You're sure."

"Yes." She tried not to focus on the heat radiating from Catherine's hand but it was impossible not to.

"Follow me." At the end of the hall, she pointed to the left. "Have a seat in the living room and we'll be ready in a bit. Do we need to bring anything?"

Avery grinned. "Just yourselves."

Avery and Polly looked around the large open space and Avery's eyes were drawn to the bouquet of daisies that set in the middle of the coffee table. The daisies she had given her yesterday. Avery had wondered if she kept them. As if Polly could sense her anxiousness, she rubbed against her leg. "Let's sit down and await our guests."

It didn't take long before Lincoln, Abigail, and Catherine stepped into the living room. Lincoln and Abigail had Harry Potter backpacks thrown over their shoulders and Catherine had a small tote bag resting on her shoulder. Where Lincoln and Abigail wore Gryffindor student uniforms, Catherine had on the same pair of black pants, but had changed into a gold Cashmere sweater and black pumps. A Hufflepuff scarf was tied loosely around her neck.

Avery's heart raced and she couldn't take her eyes

off Catherine as they walked farther into the room. She didn't know someone could be dressed so simply and still look so damn sexy. Catherine pulled it off with ease. She fought to keep the butterflies that seemed to take up permanent residence in her stomach at bay, but knew it was a lost cause, so she gave up trying to squish them. Never in a million years would she have guessed Catherine would take her suggestion to heart and dress for the party. It sent a chill down her spine and was a huge turn-on. For once, she didn't care that her desire was written all over her face. "Fantastic." She rubbed her hands together. "Everybody ready?" She had a feeling this would be a weekend she wouldn't soon forget.

※※※※

After two movies, countless snacks, and an epic battle of Trivial Pursuit and Clue, which Catherine won both by a landslide, everyone decided on pizza for dinner, even Catherine. Avery shooed everyone into the living room after the food was devoured and instructed them to start the third movie. She had just wiped off the kitchen counters when Catherine walked into the kitchen and asked her if she needed any help.

Avery threw the paper towel in her hand away. "I'm done, but thank you for offering." Avery started to fidget under Catherine's gaze. "Do you need anything?" She knew the girls were having fun and after Abigail had a talk with her about her intentions toward Catherine, the girl had reluctantly agreed to give her the benefit of the doubt, but not before telling her she would keep an eye on her. Catherine hadn't said much, preferring to sit and watch the antics of everyone around her.

Catherine took two steps in her direction and leaned down to whisper in her ear. "I would love a glass of wine."

Avery shivered as Catherine's breath tickled her ear and sucked in a breath at the smirk playing on Catherine's lips. What she wouldn't give to have this woman in her life permanently. "Who am I to deny Catherine Davenport anything?"

"Who indeed."

Avery chuckled and motioned for her to sit at the table while she poured them both a glass of wine. "I hope white's okay?"

"It's acceptable," Catherine said after a sip. "Avery, sit down. It is your apartment."

Avery took a seat opposite her, then glanced in the living room, where Lincoln and Abigail were looking at them from the couch. Avery chuckled when they both gave her a thumbs up.

Catherine shook her head. "I don't even have to ask. They are always up to something."

"I don't know Abigail all that well, but I can vouch for Lincoln. They are good kids. You're a wonderful mother."

"You think so?" She looked wistful. She ran her finger along the rim of her wine glass.

"I do. From spending time with Lincoln, and you're letting Abigail explore her hobbies this summer." Avery leaned in closer. "And, you're here." She waved her hand in the air. "You love them. It's evident."

"Thank you. What about your parents? Even after spending time with you I don't know that much about you."

Avery settled back in her chair. "I grew up in

Missouri. My dad is a dentist and my mom is a graphic designer. They were only married a year before they got divorced." She fiddled with the tablecloth. "I love my grandma, but she was a hard woman to get along with. It was her way or the highway. I could say a lot of bad things concerning her and the way she treated my mom, but I won't. She was never that way with me. I think that because of what she did to my mom, she always treated me differently. As she got older, you could tell she regretted some things and wished she could change others, but mostly she was satisfied with her life."

"Is it too personal for me to ask what she did to your mom? You don't have to answer."

"My grandparents were very rich and entitled. My mom fell in love with a poor farm boy and they eloped without my grandma's knowledge. When she found out, she was furious and told my mom if she continued with the marriage she would disown her and cut her off. My mom told me that she ignored my grandma for almost a year. When Grandma cut them off, they struggled to pay their bills, then mom found out she was pregnant with me."

Catherine nodded. "She chose you and your future."

"Yes. I resented my mom for many years when I got old enough to understand what she had done. She loved my dad, I believe she still does in her own way, but I also know she loves my stepdad, as do I. He is an amazing man. It took me a lot of years to understand what she had sacrificed for me."

"Sometimes, Avery, we make the wrong decision for the right reasons," Catherine said, with a faraway look on her face.

Avery tilted her head and wondered what hard decision Catherine had to make. "She's happy and I don't know how my life would have played out if she hadn't done what she did. I'm not saying I wouldn't have been happy, but I wanted for nothing, including love. My dad and I had a falling out when I was eighteen and my mom hasn't spoken to him since. She and my stepdad have been my safe place to go. I also have a younger brother, Daniel. I can't imagine my life without him or my stepdad." Avery breathed a sigh of relief when Catherine didn't look bored like she was expecting, but she had to ask. "I'm not boring you, am I?"

"No." She licked her lips. "The damage can't be undone by your falling out?"

Avery topped off their wine. "No. When I told them both I was gay, he didn't take it well. My mom is my rock and I don't know what I would do without her. My stepdad *is* my dad. My mom married him when I was three. Even though my dad loves me, if I was in trouble, or needed a helping hand, he would not be my first call. My mom and stepdad would be."

"Hear, hear. Avery's mom is amazing. As is her stepdad." Mia squinted at their wine glasses. She looked into the living room, then picked up Avery's glass and took a quick sip. "That's good. Don't worry, ladies, I won't tell." She grabbed three bottles of water then headed back into the living room.

Catherine looked uncertain and the last thing Avery wanted was for her to be uncomfortable. "I…"

Avery reached across the table and picked Catherine's hand up, cutting off whatever she was going to say. She caressed the back of her hand with her thumb. "I don't want you to think that you have to tell me about your family or growing up, because you don't have to. I don't want you to feel like you have to just because I did. We can talk about anything you want to." Catherine's hand was so soft.

After a few moments of silence, Catherine spoke. "Have you ever been in love?"

It was such an unexpected question; Avery took a few minutes to answer. "Yes, I have." Avery felt the sudden loss when Catherine took her hand back. She wanted to shout she was in love now, but held her tongue. It was way too soon to be declaring such things.

Catherine smiled and she had such a wistful look on her face, Avery's heart clinched painfully. "I have been in love also. We were in college and it was so easy to talk to her. It was the first time I had ever felt so comfortable with anyone in my life. After college, we went in different directions. I stayed in New York and she went to Europe."

Words escaped her at Catherine's admission. Catherine went from happy to sad in a matter of seconds. At times, she was an open book, and at other times, she was so hard to read. It frustrated Avery to no end. "That must have been hard."

Catherine nodded. "It was. I haven't seen her in twenty-five years."

"Do you want to?"

"I don't know. Wouldn't I owe it to myself to see if there was still something there if I ran into her again? To try and see if the spark was still there." She avoided Avery's eyes.

Avery hoped this was a hypothetical situation. "I don't know. Twenty-five years is a long time. People change. She might not even be the woman you remember." She didn't want to ask the question but she needed to know the answer. If only for her peace of mind. "Would you want to try again?"

"You wouldn't want a second chance with your first love?" Catherine finished off her wine, then stood up, carried both their glasses to the sink, and rinsed them out.

Avery stood up as well. "No, I wouldn't. I was different with her. I like who I am now. A lot of time, the past needs to stay the past. I've learned that the future is what you make it, and the past may present opportunities to grow, but it's the past for a reason."

Catherine opened her mouth to answer when Abigail ran into the kitchen and grabbed her mother's hand. "Your favorite part is about to come on."

Catherine looked so torn, Avery answered, "Well, let's go then." This conversation couldn't end quickly enough for her. She grabbed them each a bottle of water and handed hers to Catherine when she walked back into the living room. Avery plopped down on the floor beside Brady and curled into his side when he wrapped his arm around her shoulders, but she couldn't take her eyes off Catherine, who was curled up in the recliner with her eyes fixed on the television.

Tonight hadn't gone in the direction she had hoped and she had learned something she didn't want to. She hoped to God that it was a hypothetical situation. How in the world would she be able to compete with Catherine's first love, whom she obviously still harbored feelings for? It was a no-win situation. If Catherine's first love was back in the picture, should she give up or keep trying? Seeing Catherine and her girls so comfortable in her living room told her all she needed to know. Until that time came, she would fight for her and for them.

The weekend flew by and before she knew it, Sunday evening came around and she said her goodbyes to all three Davenport women. Her friends had taken quickly to the trio, especially when they saw them in their costumes. After their conversation Saturday afternoon, Avery had come to the revelation that she wanted to be in Catherine's life no matter the circumstances, even if that was only as a friend. She wasn't giving up on wooing her, but she would refrain from going over the top, and try and get to know her more. Maybe slow was the best option right now. She would go slow. Monday morning, she had ordered another bouquet of daisies and had them slip a Kit-Kat between the stems.

She ate breakfast with mother and daughter, then she and Lincoln settled down to work on the website. They repeated the same routine Tuesday and Wednesday morning, except for the breakfast choices. As the clock ticked by on Wednesday, Avery reached toward Lincoln and stilled her shaking leg. She realized early on that it was a nervous habit of hers, and usually it didn't bother her, but Lincoln had been doing it all morning. "You okay?"

"Would you like to eat lunch with me and Mom today?" She rushed out.

Avery bit her lip to keep from laughing at the girl's nervousness. Since the weekend, they had grown closer and even Abigail had taken to texting her occasionally. "I would love to."

Lincoln tapped her pen on top of the desk. "Good. That's good. Mom had a really good time over the weekend. Abby and I did too."

"I'm glad and for the record, so did I."

At a quarter to twelve, Catherine walked out of her office and stopped in front of Avery's desk. "Lincoln, are you ready for lunch?" Avery groaned when she realized Catherine didn't know Lincoln invited her to go with them.

Lincoln hopped up. "We're ready."

Catherine arched an eyebrow and regarded them both, but didn't object when Avery stood and followed them out the door. She could feel the stares of the other employees on them but ignored them and followed the duo out the door. Lincoln strolled ahead of them and Avery thought it was a good a time as any to say something. "I didn't realize she asked me to lunch without your permission. If it's a problem, I'll go someplace else."

Catherine stopped walking and reached for her hand. Avery's heart almost stopped beating at her first touch. "Don't be silly. It's not a problem. Over the years, I have learned to expect the unexpected from my daughters. You're always welcome to join us."

"Really?"

Catherine squeezed her hand, but didn't let go when they started walking and caught up with Lincoln, who stood outside the restaurant, waiting for them.

Lincoln rolled her eyes. "Bout time."

"Just open the door." Avery held it open for Catherine to walk through.

They strolled in and were seated right away. After their orders were placed, they sat in a comfortable silence, then Avery felt it. Catherine sat across from her, staring out the window, and was currently rubbing her foot up and down Avery's leg. Avery squirmed in her seat and received a glare from Lincoln, who was messing with her phone. She knew it wasn't her place, but the table was no place for a phone. She reached over, grabbed the phone from a protesting Lincoln, then slipped it in her bag. "After lunch, you can have it back." Lincoln narrowed her eyes, but didn't make a fuss.

As Catherine kept up her antics, Avery risked a glance at her, and even though her face was unreadable, she could see a glint in those blue eyes. "Thank you again for inviting us to join your weekend. We enjoyed ourselves." Catherine withdrew her foot when their food was placed on the table.

"You're welcome." The conversation was somewhat halted while they ate.

When their plates were cleared, Lincoln took the opportunity to speak. "I think I'm going to sign up for a pottery class. There are four classes in the first session and the first class is this coming Saturday. When I called, there were still four spots open."

"That sounds like fun." Avery handed her back her phone. "I've always wanted to try pottery."

"You could go with me. It would be nice to have someone there with me. That's when Abby's bird watchers group meets." She looked at her mom. "Mom, would it be okay if Avery went with me?"

Avery held her breath. It was one thing to spend time with Lincoln in the office, but for her and Avery to spend time together, just the two of them, would be huge. Catherine tapped her finger on the tabletop. Avery had learned that was a nervous habit of hers. She had learnt quite a bit about her on Saturday. Catherine was a lot more down to earth then she expected, and at the end of the fourth movie, she had gotten a kiss on the cheek, before they all turned in for the night.

"If Avery wants to join you, I don't mind, but it has to be her choice." Catherine started on her leg again and Avery almost hopped out of her seat.

"What is wrong with you?" Lincoln glared at her.

"Nothing," she squeaked. "And yes I would love to go with you. I don't have any plans for the next four Saturdays, if I'm not needed for work."

"I think we'll be able to manage without you for a couple of hours, Avery." Catherine looked at her over the rim of her coffee cup.

"When we get back, pull up all the information and we'll get signed up. I wonder if we will have to make what they tell us to, or if we can go rogue?"

Lincoln fist bumped her. "Rogue."

Avery laughed and took a sip of her tea. "Catherine, you don't want to join us?"

"I think I'll pass. I'll take the extra alone time and finish up some sketches I've been working on."

"Does it take you a long time to put a collection together?" Avery knew it was different for every designer, but what she'd seen from Catherine, she made it look so easy.

Lincoln didn't wait for Catherine to answer before speaking. "When Mom gets an idea, it usually doesn't take her very long to finish something. It only took her three days to sketch last year's spring collection."

"That's amazing."

Lincoln nodded. "It is. When she gets something in her head, it's hard for her to change it, no matter if she tries to avoid it or not."

Avery could feel Catherine's eyes on her even though she was looking at Lincoln. The kid was a busy body. "Well, Lincoln, that's good to know." She picked up her cup and finished her tea. Lincoln winked at her, then turned back to her mom and smiled at her.

Catherine shook her head, but her eyes danced. "If you two are finished bonding, let's head back to the office." After Catherine paid the check and they exited the restaurant, Lincoln took the opportunity and walked ahead of them to give the two women some privacy. Avery didn't think the girl could be subtle even if she tried. Catherine touched her arm, bringing Avery's focus back to her. "When do you think we'll be able to launch the new website?"

Avery ignored the lingering tingles on her arm, when Catherine removed her fingers. "The plan is to launch it next week. If you want, when we get back, I can show you what I've got. I've been in touch with the manufacturers and everyone has been helpful. I think it's going to do well. The marketing campaign should roll out Wednesday in anticipation for the big reveal."

"I would like to look at what you've done." Catherine nodded at a few people who acknowledged her on the street, but continued walking. If asked, Avery knew she would have stopped for a photo, but most people didn't have the nerve to ask her.

Avery sidestepped an old man who veered into her path, and had to grab a hold of Lincoln's shoulders to keep them both standing. "Sorry." Lincoln glared at her, then continued walking ahead of them.

Catherine snickered, slipped her hand through Avery's arm, and walked close to her. "I guess I'm going to have to keep you close by, Avery. You seem to be a danger to yourself."

Avery shivered and memorized the feel of Catherine's hand on her arm. It felt like a dream. One she didn't want to wake up from. "Well, if you must."

Catherine laughed and Lincoln turned to face them, eyes widening when she got a look at them. She quickly turned back around, but not before Avery noticed the smile on her lips. The kid wasn't so bad. Now, she had a date with the daughter; she needed to find a way to have one with her mother.

※※※※

The following day, after an enjoyable breakfast of omelets, Avery and Lincoln had gotten started on their long to-do-list. Avery looked up from her tablet, when she heard the familiar echo of Catherine's heels as she walked out of her office. Avery noticed she had several poster boards in her hands. Avery couldn't take her eyes off her as she set up two different poster boards across the room from them.

The way she walked and carried herself never failed to set Avery's heart racing. Today she wore a form fitting gray sleeveless dress that showed an insane amount of cleavage, and a tasteful gold necklace. Lincoln snickered beside her and Avery tore her eyes away from Catherine and focused on the list she was working on before being distracted.

Avery tired and failed numerous times to keep her eyes to herself, but they strayed to Catherine of their own accord. She sat up straighter when Catherine turned and headed in their direction. The sway of Catherine's hips mesmerized her as she walked closer. She leaned back in her chair and beamed up at her when she stopped in front of her desk. "Catherine."

Catherine eyed them both and motioned for them to follow her. "If you two would come with me." Without waiting, she turned and walked back to her

The Details in the Design

poster boards. Lincoln shrugged and they both stood up as not to keep Catherine waiting. She stopped them before they could see what was on the poster boards. "I have been working on a few new things and wanted to get both of your opinions on them."

That Catherine even wanted her opinion showed Avery just how far their relationship had come. She had to keep herself from bouncing up and down. "Okay," she stuttered out and Lincoln held back a laugh. Catherine rolled her eyes and motioned them around the table. As soon as Avery's eyes landed on the drawings pinned to the poster board, a wide smile broke out on her face. One poster board held several different sketches of socks, and the other board held sketches of ties. "These are awesome." She took a step closer and admired the intricate designs and bold colors that ran throughout the drawings.

"Mom, these are so cool." Lincoln ran her hand over one of the sketches.

Avery nodded as she and Lincoln stepped closer to the boards. "I love this pink and gray design." She pointed to the sketch on the left. The block style sock was eye catching and she would definitely wear the accompanying tie. "I think these would go over well. I would buy them."

Catherine beamed at them and pointed to several designs. "I was pleased with the outcome. They're not finished, of course, but I think it's a promising start. Avery, I would like to set up a plan to start putting feelers out for these. I would like to roll them out within the next six months. I wasn't planning on doing anything new, but I think it's doable." She turned to Lincoln, then reached down, picked up another board that rested against the wall, and set it in front of the ties.

Lincoln gasped beside her and gripped Avery's arm almost to the point of it being painful. "These are mine." Avery pried her fingers off her arm and scanned the poster board. There were four different sketches of messenger bags and all of them were extremely detailed, just like Catherine's drawings.

One thing was for sure. This family had talent. "Lincoln, these are good." And they were. Avery would have bought one, if she'd seen them in a store. She had watched her sketching during the day, but Lincoln would never let her see what she was doing. "Are these what you've been drawing in your down time?"

"Yes." She rubbed her neck. "I wasn't sure how good they were."

"Don't feel bad, Avery, she wouldn't show them to me until a couple of nights ago." Catherine pulled Lincoln into her side and kissed the top of her head. "Avery's right, these are good." She picked up a piece of paper and turned it over. It depicted the letter's L and D intertwined. "You should have your own label. If you don't like it, we can redesign it together?" Catherine laughed when Lincoln threw her arms around her and squeezed. "You've earned this, sweetheart."

"Mom, this is awesome. I don't know what to say."

Their laughter quieted when Camden walked up to them. Besides the three of them, he was the only one still left at the office. Avery had thought he left a couple of hours ago. He eyed the designs, and even though his face was expressionless, Avery could the tightening of his jaw. "What's going on?" He asked.

Avery crossed her arms. How could she be the only one that didn't like him? Didn't everyone else see what an asshole he was? "We're just looking at the new sketches for the new line."

He eyed Catherine, then the sketches. "I didn't think you wanted to start a menswear line?" he said accusingly.

"I'm not, but I have been wanting to delve into a few different areas. The socks and ties, along with the bags, will be unisex. I don't want to become stale." She leaned against the window.

"I see." He looked between Avery and Lincoln. "Why are they here? I would have given you my opinion."

"Avery, because she finally gave me the motivation to go in this direction, and Lincoln, because she's my daughter, but also because she's the one that designed the bags." The pride in her voice was unmistakable.

He clasped his hands behind his back. If Avery hadn't been around him the last few weeks, she would have mistaken the anger on his face for hurt. "You've always told me you would never add another person to your line."

Catherine tensed and pushed away from the window. "I don't owe you an explanation, Camden, but she isn't just anyone. She's my daughter." Catherine narrowed her eyes at him.

The tension had risen a few notches in the matter of a few seconds. It was clear Camden felt that she should have come to him, but Avery would never take his side. She didn't know why Catherine kept him around. "Catherine," Avery said. "You've sold me." Lincoln winked at her. "Kid, if your mother doesn't need us, we should finish what we were working on so we can get out of here." Catherine nodded and they both made their way back to their desk. Once she was seated, Avery peeked a glance at Catherine and Camden and their heads were bent together.

Lincoln bit her lip and fiddled with the paperclips Avery had decided to put back out, but was quickly rethinking her decision. "Avery, what do you think they're talking about?"

Avery pried the paperclips away from her and slid them back in her desk drawer. Before shutting it, she withdrew a Hershey chocolate bar and handed it to Lincoln. "Nothing good." Avery tore her eyes away from the scene in front of her, gave her undivided attention to Lincoln, and accepted half of the bar when she handed it to her "I think that he is pretty upset that your mom didn't get his input first or maybe the fact that she didn't ask him to design anything." The chocolate melted in her mouth and hit the spot.

Lincoln took a sip of water. "He didn't seem happy that she liked my designs."

"That's too bad for him. He couldn't hack it with his designs and your mom has never given him the opportunity to design for her brand. But she is right." Avery tapped the tip of Lincoln's nose. "You are her daughter, so why shouldn't she give you an opportunity? Besides, your bags are designed well and I would buy one. But, rest assured, your mom isn't giving you a chance just because you're her daughter. She wouldn't add your name to her label unless she thought you deserved it."

"I know. He needs to get over it. I've never really liked him."

Avery laughed and pulled Lincoln into a hug. "Let's get this list finished, then we can move on to more exciting things. Like dinner." Lincoln nodded, then picked up her notebook. Avery glanced back at

Catherine, who was alone, and staring back at her with a thoughtful expression on her face. Camden, thank goodness, wasn't anywhere in sight. Catherine smiled at her, then moved back to the poster boards.

It was getting harder and harder to be near the woman and not do something extremely stupid. Like push her up against the wall and kiss her senseless. She shook her head to rid herself of the inappropriate thoughts and accepted the notebook when Lincoln handed it back to her. Work now, then later in the comfort of her own bed, she could fantasize all she wanted about Catherine and what she wanted to do to her.

⁂

The rest of the week crawled by, but every day Avery ordered flowers to be delivered and every day she went to lunch with Catherine and Lincoln. On Saturday, she arrived early at Catherine's townhouse, but before she could enter, Lincoln opened the door and proceeded to shut it in Avery's face, but not before she noticed a red handbag sitting on the table in the hall. She'd never seen Catherine carry a red bag, but that didn't mean she didn't own one. Before she could ask what was up, Lincoln walked past her and down the steps to the cab.

It wasn't until they were halfway to their class that Avery voiced what she had been thinking. "Are you okay?" Lincoln fidgeted beside her.

"Fine," Lincoln mumbled and fiddled with her phone, avoiding looking in Avery's direction.

She seemed distant, which was a bit odd, but Avery waved it away as normal teenage hormones.

"I'm pretty excited for our class." After their first class, they both had opted to make a cup and a bowl.

"Me too. We should finish our bowl today."

"Yes. I figure after class we can get something to eat, and maybe ice cream, if you want to? I've already okayed it with your mom and we can pick Abigail up on the way to lunch." Avery would never take for granted the fact that Catherine trusted her with her kids. It was a gift and she would never do anything to put that at risk.

That seemed to perk her up and she finally looked up from her phone. "What flavor?"

"Mint chocolate chip. What other flavor is there? You?"

Lincoln wrinkled her nose. "Chocolate, of course, with sprinkles. Abigail prefers butter pecan."

"And your mom?"

"Vanilla."

"Of course." They fell into silence on the rest of the ride to the small studio, but once they sat down and class started, they were both too engrossed even to think about starting a conversation.

Class flew by and before she knew it, all three of them were seated for lunch. Avery had let them pick their lunch destination and they had decided on a small family owned Italian restaurant. After they ordered, she decided just to go for it.

To add to Lincoln's aloofness, when they picked Abigail up, she was also acting odd. A bit more than usual. "I know something is bothering you. What's wrong? You both can talk to me. It will stay just between us." She took a bite of her lasagna, waiting for either one of them to speak up. Lincoln and Abigail stared at each other, having another non-verbal conversation. The first time she had saw the ritual was at their weekend party and it never failed to amaze her. She waited patiently for one of them to speak up.

"It's just." Abigail bit her lip. "Mom's been so caught up in the upcoming fashion week and her new line that we haven't had much time to spend together. She's always busy. Always out." She stabbed at her French fries and dunked them dramatically in her ketchup before shoving them in her mouth.

She knew she had to be careful. This was a fine line and she didn't want to cross it. "I'm sure if you talk to her, she'll try and make some extra time for you. Your mom loves you."

Lincoln sighed. "It's not just that." She gulped and set her fork down. She ran her hand through her hair. "An old acquaintance of Mom's arrived a few days ago and they've been spending quite a bit of time together, catching up. I don't really like her." She picked her fork up and stabbed at her pasta.

Avery's heart plummeted at the term 'acquaintance.' That was usually code for an ex. That didn't bode well. Surely it wasn't the woman Catherine had mentioned at their Harry Potter weekend. What were the odds of that happening? Or, what if Catherine knew she would be seeing her again and preparing Avery for the inevitable? What if she had waited too long to make her move? She stabbed at her lasagna, then took a bite, and chewed. What if this woman swooped in and took Catherine away from her? Wooed her better. She licked her fork. "Your Mom's been spending a lot of time with her?"

They both spoke at the same time. "Yes."

She knew she could pump the girls for information, but it would only make her feel guilty.

Sometimes it sucked being an adult. She decided to avoid talk of the other woman at all. "Well, I'm sure she still doesn't realize you feel left out. Your mom is a capable woman. Just talk to her. Lay it all on the table. Give her all the options."

"You mean like you do," Abigail spat.

Leave it to Abigail to throw it back in her face. "Touché, Abigail. Touché."

"That's what I thought."

"Look," Lincoln said. "We like you. It's just a bump in the road."

Abigail glared at her sister. "It's more like a crater."

That didn't sound good. She looked between them both and wished she could decipher the looks that passed between them. "Okay. Why don't we agree that this isn't a conversation we should be having?" She waited until they both nodded. "Good. Abigail, how was your bird watchers meeting today?"

"The Winged Observers."

Avery swallowed her sip of water. "What?"

Abigail set her fork down and held Avery's eyes. "The name of our group is The Winged Observers."

"That's awesome. You should have T-shirts made. Do you have a logo?"

Abigail narrowed her eyes. "Are you making fun of me?"

"No." Avery grabbed her notebook, opened to a blank page, and scribbled a few ideas down. "It's really cool. So, T-shirts?"

Abigail shrugged, but Avery could see the interest in her eyes. "We've talked about it."

"If you would like, I can work up a logo for you."

"That would be acceptable." She picked her fork

back up.

Avery laughed and turned her attention to her sister. "Lincoln, anything new with you?"

She rolled her eyes. "You pretty much know everything that is going on with me."

Avery pointed her fork at her. "It's the pretty much part I'm wondering about." When the girl blushed, she decided to cut her some slack so she changed the subject. They discussed the latest ordeal with the website.

Avery finished her lasagna, Lincoln her penne, and Abigail her chicken sandwich and French fires, then Avery paid the bill and they headed back to the townhouse. Everyone was quiet in the ride back. Avery knew they didn't mean their offer to come inside so she waved them off. She left them with a promise to see Lincoln on Monday and Abigail next Saturday.

As the cab pulled away from the curb, Avery couldn't help but feel a sense of dread. If this was the woman from Catherine's past, what were her intentions? Avery knew what she felt, but could she compete with a woman that knew more about Catherine than she ever would? With a heavy heart, she realized the red handbag probably didn't even belong to Catherine.

As soon as she walked into the apartment, she knew her plan to be lazy for the rest of the day was shot to hell. Mia stood in the middle of the room, with her hands on her hips, eyeing the floor to ceiling windows. Avery knew that look. Mia probably had some type of home improvement scheme swimming in her head. She set her bag down by the door and paused mid-step when a spicy aroma drifted her way.

"It's pork stew." Avery screamed internally. Mia got the recipe from her mom and only made it on special occasions. Avery thought back through her memory but couldn't recall that today was anything special. She opened her mouth to speak when Mia cut her off. "Don't think too hard, Avery. Today isn't anything special, but I have recruited you and Brady to help me paint." She pointed at the far wall. She shrugged. "So, I thought I would make pork stew."

"You suck, Mia." Avery shook her head, crossed to her bedroom, and changed into a pair of cut off shorts and a ratty tank top. When she walked back into the living room, Brady had arrived, wearing an outfit like hers, but his was nice enough to be seen out in public with.

"Hey, love."

"Brady." She sighed and helped Mia lay out the drop cloth. When she raised back up, Brady handed her a candy bar.

"I thought you could use this." She didn't say anything but accepted it and tore it open, taking a bite. He wrapped his arm around her shoulders. "Do you want to talk about it?" She shook her head. "All right. So, let's get this party started."

She finished her candy bar and picked up a paintbrush. They always designated her to do the cutting in. As Mia and Brady joked around, she realized it was the perfect distraction to the unexpected news the girls had bestowed on her. This was exactly what she needed. A mindless activity to take her mind off things she couldn't change. At least, not right now.

※ ※ ※ ※

On Monday, Avery ordered her usual flowers and entered the office early, but Catherine and Lincoln weren't there yet, so she went to the bakery down the street and picked up donuts for everyone. By the time she made it back, they still hadn't arrived, so she took a donut, sat at her desk, and got started on her work.

At eight-thirty, they walked in, Catherine headed straight for her office, and Lincoln headed toward her. Her heart lifted when she noticed the red handbag clutched in Catherine's right hand. So, it didn't belong to the mystery woman after all. Good. She pointed to the kitchen. "I brought donuts if you're hungry."

Lincoln scowled. "We already ate. We ate with her."

"Oh." The grin was wiped off Avery's face.

"Yes, oh." She slapped her notebook down on the desk before sitting down.

"So, I shouldn't expect you two early for breakfast anymore?"

She bit her lip. "I don't know. Look, I know she likes you. Whoever this woman is, she will be gone in a few days. Back home, she said. She goes on and on. She never shuts up."

"You've spent time with her?" Well, that was a depressing thought.

"We've had dinner with her the last three nights."

She felt sick. This couldn't be happening. She thought for sure they were growing closer. If Catherine wasn't interested in her, what was all the footsy and holding hands about? She didn't seem like the type to play the field with multiple women. But she also understood what it was like when an ex came back into the picture, especially if they both parted on good terms.

At ten sharp, Catherine gathered everyone together for their monthly employee meeting and fifteen minutes into the meeting, two deliverymen entered. One carried the daisies she had ordered that morning and the other one carried a dozen red roses. Avery's heart sank and Lincoln sent the deliveryman with the roses a death glare. Avery had opted for all orange daises that morning. They were exquisite, but compared to the roses they lacked color and depth.

Catherine pointed the men toward her office, then resumed the meeting. When Lincoln patted Avery's hand under the conference table, she had to fight the urge not to break down. Catherine never once looked in her direction. Now she knew something was going on. She was being out wooed.

She couldn't help but glance in Catherine's office when Lincoln and she sat down at her desk to continue working. Lincoln bit the end of her pen when her mom picked up the card on the daises, read it, then set it down on the desk. Neither missed the spark in her eyes when she picked up the card for the roses and tapped the card on her lips before picking up the daisies and setting them on the table behind her desk. She pushed the roses to the corner of her desk and couldn't keep her eyes off them.

"What did you write on your card?" Lincoln asked without breaking eye contact with Catherine's office.

"Your smile brightens my day." It seemed like a good choice at the time, because her smile did brighten her day.

Lincoln nodded. "That's nice. Really nice." She looked thoughtful before jumping up. "I'm going to go see what was written on the card for the roses. We need to know what we're dealing with." Before Avery could protest, Lincoln was headed toward her mom's office.

After a few minutes, she came back and sat back down.

"What did it say?"

Lincoln looked at her funny. "Thank you for an amazing time last night."

"Oh." Well, that wasn't good. Not good at all. "Did she go out last night?" Shit. She ran her fingers through her hair.

"Yes, but I don't know who she visited." Lincoln slumped down in her seat. "I asked her why she moved the daisies but kept the roses on her desk."

"What did she say?" She was afraid of the answer.

"She said they were a sure thing, but she hadn't received roses in ages."

"I would have sent roses, but you told me daisies." She broke the pencil she held in her hand in two, then threw the pieces in the garbage. "Does she know the flowers have been from me? Be honest." Could this get any worse?

"I believe she does, but not a hundred percent. She has been flirting with you though. That's plain to see. I don't know what's going on."

"A sure thing, huh." Her confidence was quickly flying out the window.

Lincoln huffed. "Avery, don't do anything stupid. Her friend goes home tomorrow, and mom and I are going to the arts fair on Saturday. Come with us. Abigail will join us for lunch. Her bird watchers group will be meeting all morning. Or should I say the Winged Observers?"

"I don't know if that's a good idea. Not now."

"Maybe not, but at least you'll have another chance with her. I like you and Abby is warming up to you."

Avery glared at the roses. "I'm not sure how I

feel about being a consolation prize." This sucked. The pain in her chest intensified when she came to realize she and Catherine would probably be nothing but friends. She wasn't sure she could live with that, but she would have to. She took a deep breath when she heard the familiar click of heels headed their way. She watched their progress toward her desk.

"You two ready for lunch?" Catherine smiled down at them both, glowing. The roses and probably the other woman did that for her.

She tried to avoid looking at Catherine, but failed. Avery knew she would never be able to make it through lunch. "I'm not really hungry, but you ladies have fun." The frown that marred Catherine's face gave her a tiny bit of hope.

Catherine tapped her fingers on the top of the desk. "Are you sure, Avery? We don't mind you eating with us."

And the knife twisted. Were all these lunches pity lunches? Shit. Maybe she had been way off base with Catherine's feelings toward her. "I'm sure." As sure as she could be in this situation.

Lincoln stood up and closed her notebook. "Actually, Mom, I invited Avery to go with us on Saturday to the art fair after our pottery class."

Surprise flickered across Catherine's face. "Really? You've been hounding me for us time and you invited Avery?"

Lincoln stiffened and narrowed her eyes at her mom. At least one person was on her side. "Is that a problem?"

Catherine patted Lincoln's shoulder. "No, I just wanted to make sure. Avery, do you want us to bring you anything back to eat?"

"I'm good. Thanks." Catherine frowned at her again, but quickly grabbed her purse and she and Lincoln headed out. Avery snatched the last two donuts from the kitchen and ate them at her desk. She groaned when Camden took the seat beside her.

"How's it been going?"

Today he wore a gray vest over a blue button up with a black tie, and a black pair of trousers. She hated how put together he always looked. Him and his smug smile could go to hell. "Very well. Everything is on time and the website is ready to launch." She kept her eyes glued to her laptop.

He started to close her screen but she narrowed her eyes at him and swatted his hand away. "I meant about your crush."

"Like I said before. It is what it is and I won't allow my feelings to interfere with my work. Have they been?"

"No. You're excellent at your job. It's just, now she has two women sending her flowers. Just be careful. I don't want you to get hurt."

"No, you don't want my job performance to suffer," she snapped.

"You're right, I don't want it to." Camden stood up and pushed the chair into the wall. He leaned down close to her. "And make sure it doesn't. You've been spending an awful lot of time with them; just make sure that at the end of the day, you know where your place is," he said, before walking away from her.

Avery ground her teeth together and pushed back the urge to pick up the apple paperweight off the corner of her desk and hurl it in his direction. Maybe she was looking at this the wrong way? They could be just old friends. Who was she kidding? This was a nightmare. One of her own making. She should have stepped up sooner.

Today, she would feel sorry for herself; tomorrow she would get over her pity party and spend every minute with her that she could. She couldn't have a chance with her, if she didn't spend any time with her. She was just as great of a catch as the other woman. Now, she just had to show Catherine that.

※※※※

The next day after work, Avery joined Mia and Brady at a small pub a couple of blocks from their apartment building for dinner. She knew something was up as soon as she entered the establishment. It wasn't hard to deduce from the grin plastered on Brady's face. He must have come straight from work, because he still had his suit on, although she could see his tie sticking out of his pants pocket. If she had to describe him, she would say he was a cross between Matt Damon and Brad Pitt. His boyish good looks and charm had served them well over the years.

"Hey, kiddo." He accepted her hug, then kissed her on the cheek before sitting back down.

Avery looked between them both and knew exactly what this dinner was about. "Mia, I can't believe you told him."

"Avery, you out of everybody should know how hard it is to keep something from him. When he gets a whiff of something, he never lets it go."

"Whatever." After they gave their orders, Brady didn't waste any time jumping right in.

"So, Avery. What is this I hear about you having a crush on the boss? And don't be mad at Mia, I could tell there was something there at our weekend party." He tapped the side of his nose. "I am pretty observant."

Avery didn't dare look away from his gaze. She knew he was only teasing her, but she wasn't exactly in a teasing mood. "I'm not sure. Not really. Everything seems like it's happening in fast and slow motion at the same time." She buried her head in her hands.

"Avery." Mia patted her arm. "What's going on?"

Avery raised up. "When Catherine and I talked at our Harry Potter weekend, she asked me what I would do if my first love came back into my life. Would I give her another chance or not?"

Brady stood up and sat down in the seat beside her. "What's going on? You like her. Does she like you? She was cool at our weekend. At first, I wasn't sure if I would like her, but I do."

She shrugged her shoulders. "I thought she liked me. I mean, everything was adding up in that direction, then Lincoln told me that an old acquaintance of her mom's has come back into her life. One plus one makes two. I was hoping it was a hypothetical question, but now I'm pretty sure that's not the case. I think she was trying to warn me or something. I believe she has feelings for me, but now." She shrugged. "I don't know." She took a sip of her beer.

Brady winked at the waitress when she set their burgers and fries on the table. "Wow. So, let me get this straight. You get a job with the woman you've had a crush on for years. You get to know her, and she shows some signs of interest, then this other woman comes back into the picture, and you don't know what to do."

"That about sums it up."

"Well," Mia added, dipping a French fry in her ketchup and mayo mixture. "You've also been sending her flowers and gifts."

"There is that, but this other woman has started sending her roses. Compared to my flowers, the roses are like the Eifel Tower of flowers."

"You have it bad, Avery." Brady took a swig of his beer. "Tonight, you need to forget about her and just enjoy yourself. Tomorrow spend the day at home and think things through. Take Polly for a walk. What? Avery, what?"

"I have pottery classes every Saturday with one of her daughters."

Brady laughed. "So, you're not only dating the mother but also one of the daughters?"

Avery groaned. It wasn't funny. "Both girls have lunch with me every Saturday after our pottery class."

He patted her hand and encouraged her to continue. "What else?"

She did not expect to be spilling her guts tonight of all nights. "Lincoln invited me to join all three of them for a day at the art fair." She avoided looking at them both, instead opting to take a bite of her bacon cheeseburger.

"Are you sure you're not dating her?" Brady winced then glared at Mia. "You kick me again, and I'm going to kick you."

"Bring it."

"Really, you two. The girls behave better than you both do, and to answer your question, I'm pretty sure we're not dating, but it is all so confusing." She took another bite of her burger and moaned when the flavors danced on her tongue. "They have the best burgers." Brady and Mia nodded in agreement.

"What are you going to do?" Brady stole a few of her curly fries.

"Well, I'm not sure what I should do. What would you do? Would you keep on keeping on or would you let it play out at will?"

Brady held up his beer for another one. "If I really liked her, I would go for it. Life is way too short to be scared or to give up or in. If you feel there is something there, don't give up."

"You make it sound so easy."

"No, it's not easy, Avery, but if she's worth it, isn't putting your heart on the line worth it?"

He had a point, and she knew that's what he would say before they sat down. "So, how's your love life going?" He grinned then started in on his latest escapades for the next twenty minutes. When their plates where cleared, they all shared a huge piece of chocolate cake topped with cherries. She set her fork down when her phone buzzed with a new text message from Abigail. *Lincoln just informed me you were going with us to the art fair. I expect you to be on your best behavior and bring your A game. Wear something nice.* Avery couldn't hide her grin and handed the phone to Brady, who read it then proceeded to hand it to Mia.

Brady leaned back in his chair and placed his hands behind his head. "Her kids text you?"

She was almost afraid to answer the question because of the smug look on his face. "Yes."

He slipped his arm around her shoulders. "I'm afraid there is no going back for you at this point. Either push on or give up. Since she is spending time with this other woman, you have to realize she's not a hundred percent sure of her feelings for you. I don't want you to get hurt. She's more than likely figuring out where both of you fit into her life. You can't expect her to choose. At least not until she's ready. I know you would never give your first love another chance, but I would. I would love to see if what we had would still work. Don't fault her for that, Avery. Or at least try not to. You know how strong your feelings are for her, but she probably needs time to sort hers out and she is older than you." He held his hands up. "It's the truth. She's probably a bit worried about that. I know I would be. I would hope it wouldn't stop me from getting involved with someone I really cared about, but I don't know."

Avery trusted his judgement and agreed with him, but that was easier said than done, knowing that the other woman brought a smile to Catherine's eyes. She understood his reasoning. He and his first love also parted on good terms. She took another bite of cake and tried not to think about how Catherine was spending her evening. It would only torture her and she still had the rest of the week to deal with before Saturday. "I'm not really ready to go home yet." She let it hang in the air then Brady whooped beside her.

"Hell, yes. You ladies are in for a treat tonight." He grinned and finished the last bit of cake.

Mia threw her napkin at him. "Really. Because the way I remember it, we kicked your ass at air hockey the last time we played."

"Mia. Mia. Mia." Brady stood up and gestured for them to do the same. "I'm feeling it tonight." He put his hands on his chest then pointed to the door. "I bet you both fifty dollars that I'll beat you."

Avery rolled her eyes when she came back from paying their bill. "I'll take that bet. The last time I was at the pet store, I saw a couple of shirts I wanted to get for Polly. Should I say thank you now for you buying them for her?"

"Cheeky, Avery." He guided them both outside and slipped his arms around their shoulders. Avery reached up and grasped his hand. They had been friends a long time and she didn't know what she would do without either one of them. For now, she would enjoy her night and face each day as it came and try not to hold onto unreasonable expectations. Tomorrow she was sure, after work, she would be going to the pet store. Brady talked a good game, but he was always too busy staring at the waitresses to ever really pay attention to the game and she could easily beat Mia. She knew tonight wouldn't be any different.

※※※※

The following Saturday, Avery picked Lincoln up bright and early and they ate breakfast together before their morning pottery class. Lincoln informed her that the woman had left and that she point-blank asked her mom if she had slept with her. Avery choked on her water, but felt immensely better when Lincoln informed her that Catherine had said no, but she made it clear to Lincoln that she was never to ask that question again.

Maybe she had misread the situation? But her worst thoughts were confirmed when Lincoln also said that the mystery woman, who Lincoln refused to tell Avery her name, was an ex of her mother's, and they did part on good terms. It only confirmed what Avery had already been thinking, but could she fault Catherine a chance at happiness, even if it wasn't with her? Brady's words kept repeating in her mind.

After their pottery class, they walked toward the art fair and in turn toward Catherine. Avery wiped her hands on her jeans. She didn't know why she was so nervous. It was just Catherine, and Lincoln would be with her. Abigail was joining them later.

Lincoln eyed her phone. "Mom said she's by the handmade belts at the entrance."

"Lead the way." It didn't take Avery long to spot her and her breath caught in her chest when she saw her standing in front of a tree in pair of black trousers and a white, wrap around blouse.

"Breathe, Avery," Lincoln whispered before they reached Catherine.

Avery took her advice and took a minute to get her breathing under control before speaking. "Good morning, Catherine." Avery could feel the heat rise up her chest when Catherine eyed her from head to toe. Today she had opted for a pair of well-loved Levi's and a short sleeve Slytherin house T-shirt. Lincoln was dressed similarly to her.

"It is a beautiful morning."

"Well," Lincoln said. "I hate to run, but I made plans with Linda and Tara." Catherine and Avery both stared at her with stunned looks on their faces.

"Really," Avery bit out through clinched teeth. "You never mentioned this during our breakfast or our pottery class or on the walk over here." The little shit had set them up.

Catherine tensed beside her. "Nor did you mention it to me the past week, last night, or this morning."

"No big deal." Lincoln shrugged, still avoiding looking at them. "Mom, they're over there. Can I please go with them? Abigail will join me later."

"I guess." She shooed her away. "Go, before I change my mind."

"Thanks." She kissed her mom on the cheek then turned and did the same to Avery. From the look on Catherine's face, she was just as surprised as Avery, but she just shook her head and smiled. She would love to spend the rest of the day with her, but didn't know what Catherine wanted. She would let Catherine make the decision. The last thing she wanted to do was push her into something she didn't want to do.

Avery rocked back on her heels. "So?"

In answer to her question, Catherine slipped her hand through Avery's arm and told her to lead the way. She was sure Catherine would be able to hear the beating of her heart, considering it felt like it was going to beat out of her chest. She wasn't about to argue or bring up unwanted discussions; instead, she opted to enjoy the day.

They walked from one end of the fair to the other, just enjoying being in each other's company. Avery couldn't remember when she had felt so at ease with someone. She squeezed Catherine's hand that was still wrapped around her arm. "Are you hungry?" They had passed by a taco stand twice.

"Since I usually pick our destination, you pick."

"Find us a seat and I'll buy the food." Catherine nodded and walked off. Avery sighed, and stood in line, tapping her foot to the beat of the drums off in the distance. Her arm still burnt from Catherine's touch and she had to force herself not to keep touching the affected area. She didn't know if it was more torture to be with Catherine or without her. She needed to find out what was going on with her and this other woman. She bought small bowls of taco salad for each of them and sat down across from Catherine at the picnic table she had secured for them and they both dug into their meals.

Avery figured she would have to start this conversation since Catherine seemed content to sit in the silence, but she would start off with simple questions. "Who is your favorite author?"

Catherine eyed her oddly but answered. "Poe. You?"

"I don't think I have a favorite. Everybody is my favorite at the time. Favorite movie?"

"Gone with the Wind."

"Driving Ms. Daisy."

Catherine grinned and took a drink of her sweet tea. "Favorite food?"

"Tacos."

Catherine glanced at their lunch. "I should have known that."

"You?"

"French."

"Do you have a bucket list?" Avery scooped up another forkful of her salad and moaned when the flavors danced on her tongue. "What? It's really good."

"I think everybody has one. I don't have anything written down, but there are a few things I would like to accomplish before I die."

"Me too. I do have a list, though. My grandma always told me it's good to write down the things we want or things we want to do."

"I know the twins have lists and we try to do a few things a year so they can mark them off."

They both turned when a commotion to their left drew their attention. Catherine watched as a man dressed as a court jester walked by them, juggling four oranges, and Avery watched Catherine. She looked so peaceful and at ease. What she wouldn't give to lean across the table and lick the pulse point that beat on Catherine's neck. She cursed herself and quickly rid her mind of the images that suddenly overtook her. She took a large gulp of tea. "What?"

Catherine watched her for a minute then seemed to make up her mind. "Favorite place to vacation?"

"Home. Don't get me wrong, I love traveling, but there is nothing like spending a quiet few days at home. Be it by yourself or with the people you love."

"That's nice. I enjoy Greece."

"I've always wanted to go there."

Catherine looked away from her. "Give it time. You're young; I'm sure you'll get there."

Avery frowned at the tone of Catherine's voice and the tenseness of her shoulders. And there it was, the age difference. Avery groaned. What if Catherine didn't think she was serious about her because of the age difference? How could she put her mind at ease? Or what if Catherine was only interested in the other woman because they were the same age and she was afraid of taking a chance on something so unpredictable? "Catherine, I'm not that much younger than you."

"You're young enough." She stared off into the crowd, but Avery could see the tightening of her jaw.

"Only twenty years."

Catherine laughed but it wasn't a pleasant one. "That's a lifetime." She sighed. "A lifetime, Avery."

Avery reached across the table and picked her hand up, cradling it between hers. "Not really. I've never let an age difference stop me before. Some things are worth fighting for. Don't you think?"

"Yes, some things are. Others, although enjoyed in moderation, should never fully be attempted."

"You're wrong. Some things are definitely worth it. Some things are worth everything."

"Avery," Catherine started but clamped her mouth shut and pulled her hand back when her phone started ringing. She stood up, moved away from the picnic table, then answered it.

Catherine was worried about their age difference. She couldn't help but steal glances at Catherine and with every smile and laugh, her heart constricted, but to Avery's ears, the laugh seemed hollow and lifeless, like she was just running through the motions. She knew whom she was talking to. That woman. She downed the rest of her tea and stood up. By the time she had dumped their trash, Catherine had finished her call.

"Ready to see more of this fair?" Avery held out her arm and after a few moments, Catherine slipped her arm through it. At the moment, Catherine wanted her company and that was all that mattered. Today, Catherine chose her, even if she didn't realize it.

"Yes." The rest of the day flew by with plenty of laughs, food, and conversation. After an enjoyable, but simple dinner that Catherine insisted on, Avery found herself escorting Catherine home. The girls were having a sleepover at Tara's house.

The silence in the car was a comfortable distraction to the woman sitting calmly beside her. She told the cab driver to wait for her and she walked Catherine to the front door of the townhouse.

Avery slipped her hands in her jeans pockets to keep from grabbing the woman in front of her. "I had a nice time today."

"I did as well."

"Good." With heart pounding, Avery leaned forward and kissed Catherine on the cheek. She knew she had to go slow. She didn't want to freak her out. When she pulled back, a smile broke out on Catherine's face and Avery's heart melted.

Catherine grabbed the door handle, but didn't open the door. "I'll see you on Monday, Avery."

"Yes, you will." Before Catherine could answer, Avery leaned in for another kiss to Catherine's other cheek, then turned without waiting for an answer, and got in the cab.

※※※※

The next week flew by with ups and downs. Camden was still being an ass, but she had mastered the art of ignoring him without changing anything about her routine. Avery made sure to have flowers delivered at least twice a week. Catherine deserved to be pampered and she would gladly do that. Once a week, a dozen red roses would arrive, but after the first delivery, Avery couldn't have cared less.

They had eaten breakfast together every day for the last week and on Saturday, after her and Lincoln's pottery class, all three of them spent the day together laughing and getting to know each other. Little by little, she believed she was wearing her down on the age front and making her see it wasn't a big deal.

Avery leaned back in her chair, stretched her arms above her head, and glanced at the clock, surprised to see it had gotten so late. She scanned the rest of the space but she didn't see anyone except Catherine, who was seated behind her desk, staring out the window. Avery took a moment to admire the woman who had stolen her heart.

Today Catherine wore an Armani double wool

crepe jersey skirt and a Joie Marru caviar silk blouse, and Avery still didn't know how she could make something so simple look so damn sexy. It didn't hurt that Catherine wore a pair of four-inch Prada heels to complete the look. After her first week at the job, she had asked Catherine why everyone wore her designs on the day of her interview and she had told her it was more of a statement than anything else.

She bit her lip, and debated about what to do, but knew she couldn't leave without saying something to her. She didn't think they had ever been this alone before and she couldn't let this opportunity pass her by. She stood up, straightened out her sweater, slipped her heels on, and headed toward Catherine's office. She looked tired and it was only confirmed when she pinched the bridge of her nose and slowly turned toward Avery when she walked in.

Avery smiled and pointed at the chair in front of her desk. Catherine nodded and Avery took a seat. "I didn't realize it was so late and wondered if you needed anything before I left?" She held her composure when Catherine's perfume drifted her way.

Catherine bit her lip. "Isn't that my assistant's job?"

"Perhaps, but I'm here and he isn't." Avery grinned. "I don't mind staying longer if you need me to do something for you." She held her breath, but her smile vanished when Catherine started talking.

"Avery." She sighed and sat up straighter in her chair. "I'm not sure how to start this conversation. I know what's been going on the last month. Don't think I don't appreciate the flowers, and the chocolate and all the other gifts, but—"

"Stop." Avery fought the urge to flee, but knew

this was her chance to state her case. "Just answer me one question. Just one." She would not let this spiral out of control. Her heart started pounding and she fought down the urge to panic. This was not the moment for her to have an anxiety attack.

Catherine must have seen the look on her face because she relented. "All right," she said slowly.

Avery took a deep breath. She couldn't mess this up. "Do you feel anything for me?" She scooted forward in her chair. "Anything at all. Even if it's just a little smidge. I could work with a smidge." She held her thumb and index finger close together.

"Oh, Avery." She rested her head back against the chair and slipped her glasses off.

Avery shook her head. "Please don't do that. I'm just asking for a chance here. Hasn't the last month been great? I enjoy spending time with you and the girls. Please, Catherine."

Catherine sat up and slipped her glasses back on. "I'm so much older than you. This can't be what you want. I can't be what you want. Avery, I am a middle age woman, with two kids, and a cat that doesn't even like me. Not to mention that I would be considered a workaholic."

Avery shook her head. "Don't do that. Don't put words in my mouth. You are what I want. I can't change our age difference. Please don't hold that against me. Please. All I can do is show you that it doesn't matter to me. It really doesn't matter." She gripped the arms of her chair and took a deep breath. "I just want to spend time with you. I care about you. I like your kids and Polly likes cats."

"I know you care and don't think I don't see that, but I have a lot going on right now. I don't want to hurt you. Avery, for the first time in my life I am at a crossroads. I don't...I don't want you to end up getting hurt when the dust settles."

"Let me worry about that." She stood up, walked around the desk, and leaned back against it. She picked Catherine's hand up and caressed it between hers, running her thumb over her palm. "Just hear me out. Right now, that's all I am asking for." At her nod, Avery went on. "Do you have feelings for me? Real live, genuine feelings."

Another nod and Avery breathed a sigh of relief and placed a kiss on Catherine's palm. "Why don't you take some time to think about us? Give me an answer after fashion week. That's three weeks from now. Whether or not you want to move toward a relationship with me. Because that's what it will be. Not a fling, or a one-night stand, it will be a relationship. Don't let the difference in our age affect your answer." Catherine nodded. "Okay. If you decide you only want to be friends with me, it will suck, but at least I will have an answer and I will do my best not to hold it against you. I will try and be a grown up about it."

Catherine sighed and squeezed Avery's hand. "You make it very hard, Avery." She closed her eyes. Avery's insecurities started to flood in and she started to have second thoughts about her speech when Catherine opened her eyes. "All right." She nodded and bit her lip. "I can do that. I will give you an answer after fashion week." Her gaze made Avery's heart flutter. When she leaned forward, Avery's pulse quickened and chills raced down her spine. For a moment, she thought she was going to kiss her; instead, Catherine took a deep breath. "This is all a bit overwhelming for me."

"I can appreciate that. I can. This hasn't been easy for me either. I..." She frowned. "For the record, just because I am giving you time, doesn't mean we have to quit spending time together. I still expect to eat breakfast together and the occasional lunch or dinner. Of course, Lincoln and Abigail are invited."

She smiled. "Of course. My girls do have a way with words." Catherine licked her lips and Avery fought the urge to lean forward and capture them. "Oh, Avery. You have no idea the pull you have over me."

"No, but I would love the chance to find out."

"After fashion week?" She arched her eyebrow.

"Yes. And." Avery winked. "I'll wear my sexy dress for you." Avery kissed the hand she held between hers.

Catherine shuddered. "Well, how can I refuse that offer?"

"Indeed. It is not something you want to miss."

"Avery, you have to quit looking at me like that. It's hard to think when you look at me like that." She looked from Avery's lips to her eyes and Avery's pulse quickened. "Avery, stop."

Avery shook her head and slipped her hand out of Catherine's before pushing off the desk and taking a step back. She cursed her pounding heart and ran her fingers through her hair. "Okay. Okay. I'm good." She rubbed her neck and chanced a glance at Catherine, whose eyes hard turned a shade darker. "Fuck. Okay. I'll see you tomorrow."

"Perhaps." Catherine stood up and looked out the window. "If Lincoln has anything to say about it, she'll whisk you away the minute the cab pulls up."

"I...It's not just you I want, Catherine. I know you're a package deal and even though Abigail is still on the fence about me, I care about them as much as I care about you."

Catherine slowly turned toward her and licked her lips. "You have quite the way with words, Ms. Michaels." She pointed to the door. "It's getting late. We should go."

"Yes." She had to stop herself from skipping to her desk. With more patience then she felt, she gathered her things, and headed to the elevator. She didn't have to look back to know Catherine's eyes were on her. She smiled when she heard Catherine walk up behind her. When the elevator doors opened, Avery stood aside as Catherine entered and almost stopped breathing when Catherine nodded her head for her to join her.

"Anytime tonight, Avery." Catherine smirked.

Avery couldn't keep the grin off her face as she walked into the elevator and stood beside her. Catherine's answer may have been a tentative answer, but it was an answer none-the-less. And on top of that, she finally got the privilege of riding in the elevator with her.

As soon as the doors opened, Catherine walked out, but stopped so suddenly Avery almost ran into her. "Avery, let's not mention this to anyone." She pointed at the elevator. "After all, I do have a reputation to uphold."

"My lips are sealed."

"Have a good night, Avery."

Avery watched her walk away and blushed when the security guard laughed at her. "Goodnight, Charles." His laughter followed her out the door and down the sidewalk.

The next few outings they had together were tense and awkward, but that soon lead the way to their normal interactions and Avery couldn't be more thrilled. The flowers still arrived like clockwork, but Avery had decided to give Catherine her space. However, she knew everything was running too smoothly and her good mood shattered on Wednesday. Catherine and her two assistants and Lincoln were out so Avery was manning the phones when "she" called.

"Catherine Davenport Designs, this is Avery speaking, how may I help you today?" Avery leaned back in her seat and eyed Catherine's empty office.

"Is Catherine in? I need to speak to her." A woman spoke rapidly.

Avery frowned and it took a few seconds to make sense of what the woman had said. "Ms. Davenport isn't in now, but I can take a message for you."

The woman sighed. "I've tried calling her cellphone three times, with no answer. She usually always answers. I wasn't supposed to come in until next week, but I wanted to see her today."

The woman laughed and Avery got a bad feeling. This woman was her competition. This was Catherine's first love and she just wanted to get off the phone. She tried to be friendly, but knew she came off being a bit of a bitch. She couldn't help it. This woman was her competition. "I can take a message for you."

"Who is this again?"

"Avery. Do you need me to spell that for you?"

"Well, Avery, I don't like the tone of your voice and Catherine will be hearing about it."

Avery didn't like this woman and had to fight the urge to toss the phone at the nearest wall. "So, the message?"

"Tell Cat that I will call her later."

Avery rolled her eyes at the nickname. "And whom should I say is calling?"

"Her girlfriend."

Avery almost dropped the phone, but held tight it. "Very well."

"Sarah."

"What?"

"My name is Sarah."

"Very well, if that is all?" Avery didn't get an answer, only silence. On shaky legs, she stood up, ripped the post-it note off the cube, and carried it into Catherine's office. She laid it on top of her day planner so she would see it when she came in. She rubbed a hand down her face and walked back to her desk, flopping down in her chair. Her girlfriend. Catherine had a girlfriend.

Why didn't she tell her or why didn't the girls tell her it had escalated this far before she made an ass out of herself? The last thing she wanted to do was come between two people who were already in a relationship. All the signs were there, she just refused to see them, but now she did. Quite clearly, in fact. Why was Catherine playing with her?

The minute she heard the click of Catherine's heels on the wooden floor, her heart started to race and she watched them all file back in. Catherine went straight to her office, picked up the note, and smiled. After gathering her things, Catherine walked back out of her office, informed everyone she was leaving for the rest of the day, told Lincoln the car would be back later for her, then walked out. She never once glanced Avery's way, even though she had to have known she was the one that took down the note.

For the rest of the day, she ignored Lincoln's questions and she finally got a clue to stop asking them. That night when she got home, Mia was waiting for her with a glass of wine and homemade beef stew. "Do you want to talk about it?" Mia asked after they had eaten. "You look like someone stole your puppy." They both relaxed on the couch with Polly curled up in a ball in between them.

Avery mindlessly petted Polly's stomach. "Not stole. It can't be stolen if you never had it to begin with."

"Oh, shit. What happened?" Mia jumped up and went into the kitchen, returning shortly with the bottle of wine. "I thought things were going well after you two talked and she agreed to wait until after fashion week to make a decision."

"I was left for about an hour today by myself to answer the phones and then Catherine's girlfriend called asking if I knew where she was."

Mia topped off her wine. "Girlfriend? Ouch. Wait, I thought Hannah answered the phones?"

"Not Catherine's line. It figures the day everyone leaves, I would have to take her call." She drained her glass and handed it to Mia to refill.

"Okay," she said handing her back a full glass.

"I can only assume the woman I talked to is the one that's been sending her the roses. Her first love."

"Well, fuck."

"Yes."

"Are you sure it's as bleak as you think? You did give her until after fashion week. Maybe she needs this time to sort between her feelings for you and this other woman."

"I know. I've thought about that, but after she read the note, she gathered her things and left." She hiccupped. "This sucks. I didn't expect it to hurt this much. Stupid crush."

Mia picked a protesting Polly up and set her on the floor before sitting beside Avery and pulling her into her side. "Avery, we both know it's much more than that."

Avery relaxed in her embrace and took a sip of her wine. "I just wish what I wanted mattered. If she didn't want me, she should have just told me. Instead, she gave me false hope. What the hell am I supposed to do with that?" She drained her glass, set it on the coffee table, then curled back up against Mia. "I can't stay there. Not now. After fashion week, I'll put in my two weeks."

"Are you sure that's the right move? I know what you're going through now, but in a few days, maybe your stance will have changed."

"Maybe, but she'll still have a girlfriend. It's the only choice I can make. She flirts with me, holds my hand, comforts me, laughs with me, yet she fixates on the age difference. I don't think I could handle it, seeing that woman, Sarah, come into the office and interact with Catherine."

Mia moved to the other end of the couch. "Give me your feet." They sat in relative silence until Avery's phone beeped, indicating a text message. Mia picked it up then handed it to Avery. "It's from Catherine."

Avery didn't take it. "That's another thing, Sarah called her Cat. I have never heard anyone call her that. Not even the girls." She huffed and wiggled her fingers. "Give me the phone." She read it twice then groaned.

"What is it?"

"Shit, I completely forgot. The guest bloggers are going very well, but I asked Catherine weeks ago if I could interview her for our blog and she just informed me we could do that tomorrow."

Mia patted her feet. "You've got this." They both looked to the floor when Polly started whining. Mia was always the first to give in and tonight was no exception. She picked her up and handed her to Avery, who cuddled her to her chest.

"How am I supposed to face her knowing what I do, and knowing she knows I know, while I am hopelessly in love with her? How did my boring life suddenly become so complicated?"

"I can't answer that for you, but you're a professional. So, act like one. You will knock the interview out of the park."

"I know," she said with more confidence then she felt. "I can do this."

"Yes, you can, and it doesn't matter if you can do it or not because you don't have a choice. Avery, listen. You're the one that's given her time. You can't fault her for that."

"I know. I really do, but it still hurts."

"You just expected her to choose you?"

She sighed. "I was hoping she would, yes."

"It's not always that easy, Avery. Life isn't a fairy tale and if ours were, it wouldn't be a Disney one. Don't beat yourself up. Life has a way of working out for everyone involved."

Avery bit her lip then swung her legs around and off the couch. "You really think so?"

"I do."

Avery picked up her phone. "I believe tonight is one of those nights."

Mia squealed and grabbed her phone off the coffee table. "Fantastic." She shut up from the glare Avery sent her way. "Not because you're hurting, but, you know, because."

"I get it. You call Brady, and I'll call the bakery on the corner and put our order in. Tell him to pick it up on his way over." Forty minutes later, all three of them sat on the couch, with their feet propped up on the coffee table, each with a small bakery box that contained an individual cheesecake in their hands.

She savored the first bite of hers and leaned into Brady. The creamy texture of the cheesecake combined with the strawberry reduction melted in her mouth. No matter what happened, no matter where things with Catherine would lead her, she knew there was always someone she could count on. Or in her case two someones. She smiled and laughed, despite her horrible day, when Brady stuck his fork in her cheesecake and took a huge bite.

"Do you want to talk about it?" He asked after he swallowed it.

"No."

"Fair enough. Let's enjoy our dessert and watch whatever is on the first channel I turn to." In the end, the cheesecake was heavenly, as usual, but the documentary on fire ants, while interesting, left a lot to be desired.

※ ※ ※ ※

The next day arrived much too quickly for Avery's liking, but she arrived on time so she could eat breakfast with Lincoln and Catherine. She was only slightly relieved they hadn't arrived yet, and frowned when they didn't arrive until a quarter till ten. Which wasn't unheard of but it was a bit unusual. Catherine walked straight for her office and Lincoln stopped short of running into Avery's desk, then sat down in her chair.

"You okay?" Avery asked.

"We," she pointed to the office. "Had a pretty big fight yesterday, after that woman left last night."

"Sarah, her name is Sarah. I was the one that took the message." Avery tapped her pen on the desk.

"Yes, Sarah," she sneered. "I don't like her, but she isn't a bad person. I just think Mom is happy that she's back in her life. After a tense dinner, Sarah explained to me why they broke up. It was mutual. They both were going in different directions in life." She shot a glance at Avery.

"So, I can assume Sarah still loves your mom."

"I think that's a good assumption."

She knew that, but it still sucked to get confirmation. Everything sucked. She shouldn't have even gotten out of bed that morning. "Well, there's nothing that can be done about that."

"You're taking this awful well. I thought you cared about Mom?"

"I do care, Lincoln. More than I should, actually. I've had a crush on her for years, but after I started working here, it blossomed into something I never expected. Something that will be hard to get over."

"You sound like you're giving up. Mom and I talked about you also. I know about after fashion week. Our argument was about that. I told her she shouldn't throw all her eggs in one basket, she told me to mind my own business. We screamed and I threw a few things and here we are. Abigail just stood back and watched everything, but when we went up to our rooms, she told me you were the lesser of two evils."

Avery gripped Lincoln's forearm and got her attention. "Please don't fight with your mom because of me. Things were going well and I know she's scared because of the age difference and maybe I shouldn't have given her a timeline. I don't know, but I did and she's taking this time and spending it with Sarah. It would have been nice to know that Sarah was her girlfriend and not just a friend." She stared pointedly at Lincoln, but Lincoln only frowned.

Lincoln gulped. "Girlfriend?"

"That's what Sarah said on the phone when she called. I love your mom, but I would feel guilty fighting for her, when she clearly wants Sarah right now and is happy with her. I think today's flower delivery will be the last from me."

Lincoln stared at her for what seemed like a lifetime, then she leaned in close. "You said you love her."

"What?" No, she didn't, but when she rewound what she had said, she cringed. That was the last confession she wanted to make. She waved her hand in the air. "Slip of the tongue."

Lincoln gripped her hand. "You can't give up now. Please, you do make mom happy. She's just in a weird place right now. I don't think she's ever had two women vying for her attention like this before."

"I understand that, but tell me something? Would you pick a much younger woman who offers many unknowns or would you pick a sure thing? I'm guessing your mom is the type to pick a sure thing."

"She is, but don't give up. We've come too far to let this crash and burn."

"We?"

"Yes, we. I like you and I think you'll be a much better fit than Sarah for Mom."

"I'll think about it. First, I have to get through this interview with your mom." Not five minutes later Catherine called her into her office. She set about setting up the recording device and pulled out her notebook with her list of questions. "Ready?" Avery couldn't help but notice that the atmosphere was quite tense and she tried to relax, but knew she wouldn't be able to. Not with everything rolling around in her mind. She kept repeating the mantra in her mind: Catherine has a girlfriend; Catherine has a girlfriend.

"Avery," Catherine laid her hand on top of hers, but Avery jerked it back. Hurt flashed across Catherine's face, but Avery couldn't focus on that. Her hand burned from Catherine's touch. She wasn't sure she could do this. "Are you all right?"

Avery sucked in a breath at the less than friendly tone of Catherine's voice. She was sure she was seeing her work persona right now. Maybe if she had seen this one from the beginning she wouldn't have fallen in love with her, but this is exactly what she needed to get through this meeting. "Yes. Shall we begin?"

Catherine sat ridged in her chair. "You have the list of questions."

Nope, Avery was wrong; her work persona sent the same chills down her spine. "So I do." After an hour and the final questions were answered, Catherine clicked the device off and held it out to Avery. Without touching her fingers, she accepted it, and slipped it in her bag.

"Avery, are you sure you are all right?"

She would never tire of hearing her voice. She

chanced a glance up and saw only concern marring those blue eyes. "I will be."

"Are you ill?"

She smiled sadly. "No." She knew what she promised Lincoln but looking at Catherine now, knowing she was with Sarah, probably had sex with her, let her kiss her, tore her up inside. That was supposed to be her. "But, rest assured, my job performance will not suffer."

Catherine flinched. "I'm not worried about your job. I'm worried about you." Her face showed only sincerity, but to Avery it was a false kind of hope.

"Don't. I am fine. Nothing countless other people haven't gone through. I'll live."

"You'll live? Avery, look, I…"

Avery ran her fingers through her hair. "Please, if it isn't related to the job, can I go back to work?"

"So, that's how you want this to be?" She pointed between them. "Us to be?"

Wait. What? "Us?" She leaned forward in her chair and kept her voice low. "I wasn't aware there was an us. Unless you're talking about being friends, then you'll have to give me a bit of time to adjust to that, because the way I feel, friendship is the last thing on my mind."

Catherine sighed and leaned forward also. "Friends. I thought you had given me until after fashion week to decide?"

Avery chuckled and Catherine drew back. "We both know you don't need that time." She pointed at her. "You should have been honest with me instead of treating me like your damn girlfriend when you already had one. I at least deserved that much consideration."

"What are you talking about? I don't have a

girlfriend."

"Really. Does Sarah ring any bells?"

Her eyes widened. "Avery."

"Yes, everyone sees the way your eyes light up when the roses she sends are delivered or when you get a phone call or a text message from her. You smile and laugh and it's great to see you happy, but it hurts. She just came back into your life and I know you have history, but I've been here." She shook her head. "I don't want to talk about this."

"You don't know me, Avery. Don't sit there and pretend like you do."

"You're right; I don't. That privilege falls to Sarah."

"You're right; it does."

Avery felt like she'd just been slapped. So, there it was. Fuck. She gripped the edge of the chair and closed her eyes, but her chest felt like it was closing in on itself. In and out, in and out. If she could just get her breathing under control. She tensed but instantly softened when a warm hand started stroking her back.

"Avery, calm down. Deep breath in, deep breath out."

When her breaths finally evened out, she jumped up from her chair and away from Catherine, who had a look mixed with sadness and regret across her face. "I'm fine."

"No," she shook her head. "You're not."

"I would like to get back to work."

"Okay."

Avery avoided touching her and soon found herself back at her desk and a worried Lincoln by her side.

"I take it didn't go well?"

"Your mother likes me, but I don't see it going any farther. I don't know what else I could do. Sarah knows her, she made that quite clear, and I don't."

"You know more than you think you do. Sarah is a vegetarian."

"So?"

"Mom refused to go to the restaurant she picked out last night."

"What does that have to do with anything?"

"She refused, Avery. Mom's scared. That much is obvious. She does have feelings for you, I can tell and so can you. Sarah is comfortable for her, but you, you're scary. Mom doesn't deal well with scary."

She groaned and lay her forehead on her desk. "Lincoln?"

"Avery, she refused to go to the vegetarian place. Instead we went to Mike's steakhouse."

Avery peeked up from her desk. "Really?"

"She does like you." She rubbed Avery's back. "We'll get through this. Don't look, but she's looking at us."

"Great."

"We're having a staring contest. I can see her resolve failing. There it is. She's back at her desk and your flowers are here. I think you should keep sending them, at least until after fashion week. Show her that she has a choice, that you are the *right* choice."

Avery sat up and smiled at the deliveryman as he walked by, but refused to look in the office across from hers; instead, she turned toward Lincoln. "I like you and your sister. I hope that no matter what happens, we will still keep in touch."

"That sounds ominous."

"No, just reality."

"All right. Don't do anything stupid."

"I'll try not to." Avery laughed, but her heart was breaking and she didn't know how to fix it.

※ ※ ※ ※

That night instead of drowning her sorrows in a bottle of wine at home, she and Mia went out to dinner. They had invited Brady but he had prior arrangements. She had read Todd's food column the previous day and decided to try out an up and coming restaurant. The good thing about working for Todd was that people remembered her and the maître d at this restaurant used to work for one she frequented quite a lot in her previous job.

"Avery." He kissed her cheeks. "Right this way, my dear."

"Thank you, Carmen." The restaurant was modern and sleek, but with a rustic edge. As the passed by the tables, she couldn't stop her stomach from grumbling and Carmen winked at her.

"You are in for a treat tonight." He held out first her chair, then Mia's. As they got settled, her eyes scanned the area, only to stop abruptly and widen when her gaze locked with none other than Catherine's, who sat across from a very stylish and put together woman. Sarah, she would presume. She tore her gaze away and groaned.

"What?" Mia looked up from her menu.

"Catherine is here with her girlfriend."

"Shit, seriously?" Mia laughed. "The universe obviously hates you right now."

"Yes. God, and she looks like Helen Mirren. How am I supposed to compete with that? They look amazing together." She smiled when the waiter returned with their choice of wine for the evening and took their dinner orders. "Don't look."

"Stop." Mia glanced their way then back. "Too bad she knows who I am. If she didn't, we could have some fun." Mia ran her finger down Avery's cheek.

Avery, in turn, rolled her eyes. "Stop." She swatted her hand away.

"Don't do this to yourself, Avery. You're worth more than five Sarahs put together."

"You're right. Let's just enjoy tonight." In short order, the waiter deposited their first course in front of them, Zucchini Carpaccio. Avery took a bite and let the flavors dance on her tongue. The lemon made everything pop. "That's good."

Mia took a sip of her wine. "I didn't think I would like it, but it's amazing."

Avery didn't think they would make it through all six courses, but she tore into her Buffalo, with rosemary gnocchi, and glazed sweet onions with gusto. This course, the fourth one, was by far her favorite. After swallowing, she opened her mouth to accept Mia's fork and try her Venison and parsley root. It was almost as good as hers. "We'll have to come here again. The food is phenomenal."

Mia thanked the waiter when he refilled their wine glasses. "Definitely. There are so many choices."

For the fifth course, they had both chosen the Chilled coconut soup with pineapple granite, and amaretto ice cream. Avery patted her stomach when their bowls were taken away. "That was the best meal I've had in months." They were enjoying their wine when Avery groaned, noticing Catherine and Sarah walking their way. She prayed they wouldn't stop, but her prayer was quickly rejected when they stopped right beside their table. It was hard not to notice the way Sarah's arm curved around Catherine's waist, drawing her close. She almost regretted coming here. Almost.

"Good evening," Catherine said, and by the tone of her voice, she was just as happy about stopping at their table as Avery was that they stopped. "I hope your meal was as lovely as ours was." Avery tried to smile, but was sure it came out more like a grimace.

Sarah cocked her head. "I just had to stop at this table and see what has had my Cat's attention all evening." Avery bit back the answer that lay on the tip of her tongue at the possessiveness in her words.

"Sarah, this is Avery, one of my employees, and Mia, her roommate."

"My, my, so you are the infamous Avery." Sarah looked her up and down.

"Since I was born." She downed the rest of her wine.

"With Catherine going on and on about you, I felt a bit threatened, but seeing you in front of me, I realize my fears were misplaced." She flicked her hand in Avery's direction and the gold bangle on her wrist jiggled at her.

"Sarah," Catherine said in a warning.

"No, no, Catherine, it's quite all right. Avery, you're nothing more than a kid. Probably still fantasizing about changing the world. What could you have to offer a woman who has seen the world, captured the world, and if she wanted, has the money to buy part of the world? No, my dear, I was way off base with thinking you were a threat to me."

"Ladies." A woman in a chef's coat walked up to

the table and Avery stood up when she realized whom it was and engulfed her in a hug, thankful for the reprieve. The woman held on a bit longer than precedent and Avery caught the frown on Catherine's face. Right at this moment, Avery didn't care; Catherine didn't have to stop at their table and she was here with a date, after all.

Avery smiled at her. "Sally, I didn't know you were the head chef here."

"For about three months now and when Carmen told me who was dining with us tonight, I just had to come say hello. So, hello, Avery. It is so good to see you again. I hope you enjoyed our tasting menu."

"It's was by far the best thing I've put in my mouth in months." Avery could feel the blush rising in her cheeks, but was feeling far too relaxed to care. She and Sally had met on numerous occasions when she worked for Todd, but they never got the chance to explore the chemistry between them. "It's good to see you as well. Oh," she pointed to Mia. "This is my roommate, Mia, and this is Catherine Davenport, my current boss, and Sarah."

"Ladies." She nodded at them. "Avery, I know you have one course left, but if you would allow me to change it up a bit. I have a special dessert selection for you and Mia." She winked at her. "I seem to recall you have a fondness for chocolate."

"I'm pretty full, but I can never say no to chocolate."

"I will send it out in a few minutes. Along with a dessert wine. I just wanted to come see you." She squeezed Avery's hands.

"Thank you and I'm sure whatever you have for us will be well worth it."

"Have I ever disappointed you before?" She smirked.

"Never."

"And I don't intend to now." She handed Avery a business card. "I would love to have a drink with you some time."

"That sounds nice." And it did sound nice. At least Sally wanted her and was very attractive. She kept her blond hair put up in a bun, but her classic features always set Avery's heart racing.

"Until then."

After she walked away, Mia grabbed the card from her hand. "Oh, look Avery, she wrote her personal number on the back for you. That's fantastic." She handed the card back and looked at Catherine. "You deserve someone who treats you like you're the only thing that matters to them and not be played with." Catherine flinched at the words.

"Mia." Avery sat back down. "Catherine, I hope you enjoyed your meal, also. It was quite the treat."

"Yes, it was."

Sarah looked between them both. "Tell me, Avery. How long have you had reservations? I made ours two weeks ago. It's amazing what strings can be pulled when you know the right people."

Avery smiled. "Actually, I didn't make reservations. I just walked right in."

"You're lying."

Mia took that moment to interrupt. "We just walked in. Avery still has connections from when she worked for Todd Richards."

Catherine squeezed Sarah's hand on her waist. "I guess that is all you would have to do. I'll keep that in mind."

"You do that. If there's any place you would like to eat, just let me know and I'll see if I can make it happen."

"That won't be necessary," Sarah cut in.

Mia held her hand up before Avery could comment. "Ladies, it looks like our dessert is coming. I'm sure you both have better things to do then stand by and watch us eat."

"We do, Mia," Sarah said. "Come along, Cat. I do believe you made an offer of dessert at your place."

"Avery," Mia said, after they walked away. "Don't look so sad. You should have seen the look on Catherine's face when Sally hugged you. I'm not going to lie though; I don't like the way she's treating you. You deserve better than that."

"I know. I can't help my feelings though. One thing is for sure." She stabbed her fork into the delicate pastry. "Sarah is an A-class bitch and even if it's not with me, Catherine deserves so much better."

"Let's enjoy this amazing dessert, then we'll work on another game plan."

"No more game plans for me. I've been the only one trying, and since she said receiving the daises were a sure thing, I won't be having them delivered anymore. I have given and gave and now I need to take a step back. From now until after fashion week, I will do my best to distance myself from her. If she wants me after fashion week, I will be willing and ready to give her another chance if she gives Sarah up for good. Until then, I will do my job, come home to you and Polly, and try not to worry about the outcome."

"I can drink to that."

A week after the restaurant incident, Avery could have pulled out what little hair she had. Every day Catherine had asked her to lunch and every day she had turned her down. Avery even stopped coming into the office early to eat breakfast with them. She and Lincoln still worked together, but Avery could feel the strain on their relationship.

As she promised herself she would, she stopped ordering flowers. At Mia's insistence, she had called Sally and they had plans to get together later for drinks. She was looking forward to getting out of the house, but she still felt uneasy about the situation. She couldn't deny her feelings for Catherine, and she didn't want to lead Sally on, but it would be nice to be around a woman that wanted her.

She looked up from her laptop when Catherine and Lincoln returned from lunch but didn't acknowledge them, opting to go back to the document she had been working on. What she couldn't ignore was Lincoln scooting her chair closer to hers and leaning in so their faces were almost touching. "You quit sending flowers," Lincoln accused.

"I did."

"Why?"

"Your mom still got her roses this week and she seemed pleased by them. She didn't need my flowers too."

"You don't know what she needs," she spat.

At that, Avery turned her head to look at the young woman. "You're right, I don't."

"She mentioned she saw you at the restaurant when she was out with Sarah."

"She did?"

"And that the chef was all over you."

Avery laughed. "We hugged. Big deal. I know her from my time working with Todd."

"Good. So, you won't be calling her up then?"

"Actually, I am having drinks with her tonight."

"What about Mom?"

"Lincoln, what about her? She can live her life, but I have to be stuck in a loop caring about her. It's just drinks and I am allowed. Did your mom say anything about Sarah, about the fact that she was a total bitch to me?"

Lincoln licked her lips. "No."

"Honey, to your mom, Sarah can do no wrong. She's the woman that got away and came back. She didn't try and defend me; she just stood there, like she always does."

"Mom doesn't like to make a scene in public if it can be avoided."

"That much is obvious."

"She's been sad this past week. You're pulling away from us. You're different. Even Abigail has noticed a difference in her and you."

"I'm just being me."

"No, you're not. You're sad too, you just don't want to show it, so you're pushing us away. Outside of work we haven't spent any time together."

"I've been working long hours."

"I guess."

"We still have our pottery class tomorrow."

"Our last one." After the first four classes, they had signed up for another three additional classes.

"True." What did Lincoln want from her? She could only take so much.

"Do you want to do something afterwards?"

"Just the two of us."

She shook her head. "Mom and Abigail too."

"No." Out of the corner of her eye, she saw Catherine stand up and head in their direction.

Catherine stopped in front of her desk and fiddled with the belt around her waist. "Avery, I was wondering if you would like to have dinner with us tonight?"

It took her a few minutes to answer before the shock wore off at the question. "Will Sarah be there?" The words were out of her mouth before she could censor them, but she had to know.

Surprise flitted across her features. "No, she left this afternoon."

"And you've had dinner with her every day this week?" Keeping her temper in check was staring to become a losing battle.

Catherine frowned. "Yes."

"So I'm backup. How nice." She couldn't help the disdain that crept into her voice.

"No, never." Catherine backed up a step. "Avery?"

"Don't, I shouldn't have said anything. It's clear what I want doesn't matter anyway. Besides, I have a date tonight."

"That chef."

Avery stood up. "Her name is Sally and yes. We've never had the opportunity to get together before because one or both of us had other obligations, but now we're both single, so what could it hurt?"

"You don't love her."

"What's love got to do with anything?"

"Everything."

"Thank you for the dinner invitation, but I have to pass."

"Very well." Catherine walked back to her office.

"Wait, Mom." Lincoln threw her things in her backpack and slung it over her shoulder. She leaned in close so only Avery could hear her. "Who's being the bitch now?" She walked toward her mother. "I figured I would spend the rest of the day with you."

"Of course. I always love having you in my space and you can work on the designs for the messenger bag."

If Avery didn't have several more hours of work, she would have got up and walked out. Why did she have to be the bad guy? Catherine didn't want her. She saw the hurt cross Catherine's face, but why was it that only her feelings mattered? Seeing a jealous Catherine was nice, but she wasn't sure if it was too late for them or not. Catherine was dating Sarah. Why should she feel guilty about going out with Sally?

She shouldn't have given her a timeline. The thought had crossed her mind that Catherine would spend that time with Sarah, but seeing the reality of the situation sucked. In a way, she was glad she was giving them a chance, because if Catherine came to her, it would be her choice. It would have to be. Avery had already given so much already.

After a rather long, but productive evening, she left work at nine o'clock. Catherine and Lincoln had left around five, but Avery stayed to catch up. Fifteen minutes late for her date, she entered the bar and slid onto the stool beside Sally "Thank you for giving me your card."

"Are you kidding me? It was my pleasure." Sally squeezed her hand then motioned to the bartender.

After twenty minutes of small talk, Sally leaned forward, but at the last second, Avery turned her head so Sally kissed her cheek. She knew this was a bad idea. She shook her head and Sally nodded at her. "I'm sorry. I...I thought I could do this." She ran her fingers through her hair.

Sally threw back the rest of her drink. "There's someone else?"

"It's complicated. I thought I could do this," she repeated. "There's someone else for her. I thought I had a chance, then everything went weird."

"You love her." Avery nodded and Sally motioned for another drink, but her finger stilled in the air and she spun back around to face Avery. "Catherine Davenport." She shook her head. "I should have seen that coming the way you two were looking at each other." She lifted her glass in the air. "It looks like our time has passed this time too. Avery, we're ships passing in the night."

She would have never been able to start anything with her, not with her heart tied up with Catherine. The last thing she wanted to do was hurt her. "I believe we are. Friends?"

Sally tapped her glass with Avery's. "Friends."

One drink soon turned into two, then three. It was nice being with Sally and the buzz she had started to sport didn't hurt either, that is, until her phone started ringing. After the ringing stopped, it started again, then again. A quick glance at her phone confirmed it was Catherine calling. Whatever Catherine wanted, it could wait until Monday.

Sally peered at the screen. "Maybe you should answer that? It could be important."

Maybe she should. It was unlike Catherine to call three times in a row, but upon further inspection, she noticed it was Mia's number this time. "Hello."

"Avery, where are you?" She sounded panicked and Avery got a very bad feeling. She sobered up quickly.

"At the bar with Sally."

The line was so silent she thought Mia had hung up until she spoke again. "Catherine tried calling you. Then she called me."

Avery rolled her eyes. "It can wait until Monday." Avery motioned for another drink.

"No, Avery, it can't."

Mia never used that tone with her. "What's wrong?" She waved the drink and Sally's questions away. Whatever Mia was about to say, she knew she wouldn't like it. She knew deep down when she answered the phone that Mia wouldn't have been calling unless it was something important.

"It's Lincoln."

Her grip tightened on the phone and she took several deep breaths to calm herself, but she couldn't stop the pounding of her heart. "What about her?" She frowned when Sally handed her a napkin and for the first time she realized she was crying. She wiped her eyes and waited for Mia to say something.

"She was out with friends tonight. Abigail stayed home. Catherine said Lincoln had been upset all day." She took a deep breath. "Avery, I don't know how say this."

"Just spit it out."

"The town car her and her friends were in was struck by a drunk driver."

᎒᎒᎒᎒

Avery took a deep breath and didn't shake off

Sally's hand when she gripped her arm. This couldn't be happening. "Oh my god. Is…is Lincoln all right?"

"She's alive, but in pretty bad shape. Catherine knows how close you two have gotten and she was calling to let you know." She sighed. "Listen, Avery. I know you're having a hard time dealing with your feelings for Catherine right now, and I insisted you call Sally, but you should go be with her. Her daughter almost died. The least you can do is go and offer her support. Be her friend."

She couldn't believe this was happening. "Okay."

"Okay. I am going to grab you a change of clothes and I'll meet you at the hospital."

"Thank you." She ended the call. "I have to go."

"Of course."

Sally escorted her outside and hailed her a cab. Avery kissed her on the cheek and promised her she would keep her updated. Before she knew what was happening, she was on her way to the hospital. She was sober now. A sob tore from her lips and she wiped feverishly at her eyes. The last thing Catherine and Abigail needed right now was for her to fall apart on them. Oh, God, Abigail. What must she be going through? Her feelings were all over the place; she couldn't even imagine what they were feeling. She needed to be strong for them.

She gripped her phone and watched the night fly by. The closer they got to the hospital, the calmer she became. When she got home, she could lose it when she laid down in her bed for the night, but now there were others counting on her. Catherine and Abigail were counting on her. As the cab came to a stop, she paid her fee, and climbed out on shaky legs.

At the entrance to the emergency room, she

walked in and instantly spotted Catherine huddled in the corner of the room. Abigail was seated beside her with her head in her hands. Catherine's hand was rubbing her back soothingly. Even from her distance away, she could see Catherine's eyes were red from crying. Avery's steps faltered when she spotted Sarah seated to Catherine's left. She thought she had gone home. The thought did cross her mind to leave, but then she quickly dismissed that notion. She had just as much right to be here as Sarah did. Camden waved from his seat beside Abigail and patted the seat beside him.

"You can sit here," he said.

Avery ignored him and walked up to Catherine, who looked like she was about to break down. She was being strong for Abigail, but who was being strong for her? Sarah spared her a quick glance then went back to messing with her phone.

Avery dropped to her knees in front of Catherine and without asking permission or without second-guessing herself, she leaned forward, wrapped her arms around her, and pulled her into an embrace. Catherine stiffened momentarily, but quickly relaxed and Avery held her tighter when Catherine started to cry. It tore at her heart when Catherine's left arm clung to her and she buried her head in Catherine's hair. A second later, she felt another body squat next to her and two arms wrap around her waist. Avery tightened her hold around Abigail when she buried her head in her neck and started crying.

Catherine whispered in Avery's ear. "What will I do if she dies? My baby," she choked out.

Avery leaned back so she could see Catherine's face and wiped the tears from her eyes. "Don't talk like that. We know how stubborn she is. She'll be okay." Catherine loosened her hold and nodded. Avery sucked in a breath when Catherine reached toward her and wiped her tears away.

"I have a hard time not believing anything you say to me. Why is that, Avery?" She sniffled.

"I think I just have that type of face." She smiled at Catherine and got a tentative one in return. Then Catherine noticed how Abigail clung to Avery. Avery pulled away from Abigail so she could talk to her. "Look at me. She's going to be okay."

Abigail hiccupped. "I don't know." She wiped furiously at her tears.

"Sweetheart. We are not going to lose her. Not going to happen. Trust me."

After a few beats, Abigail kissed Avery on the cheek. "Okay."

"Okay." They both stood up and Abigail told Avery she could have her seat. Camden scooted down so Abigail could have his. When Avery sat down, Abigail curled up beside her and laid her head on her shoulder. Catherine watched the scene unfold with an unreadable expression on her face. Avery reached over and tangled her hand with Catherine's. Almost instantly, Catherine squeezed it back.

Catherine turned fully toward her. "I'm sorry. For everything. I…" She rubbed her eyes. "I have held back because of a lot of factors. Yet, you always seem to be at the forefront of my mind. You're the first person I called."

Avery felt even worse now that she hadn't answered, seeing Catherine looking so broken in front of her. It was the first time she had ever seen her look so ordinary. She completely ignored Sarah glaring at her. "I'm sorry I didn't answer. You can be sure that won't ever happen again."

"You've never lied to me." Catherine rested her forehead against Avery's.

"No, I haven't, and I don't plan on starting."

Catherine pulled away from her. "Good."

The spell that seemed to surround them was broken when Mia walked in, carrying a small backpack. "Avery," Mia said. "I've brought you a change of clothes and a few snacks and drinks."

Catherine accepted the tissues Avery handed her and Avery grabbed onto Mia's hand and stood up. She tilted Catherine's head back. "I'll be back in a few minutes." She kissed her on the cheek then kissed Abigail's and followed Mia to the restroom.

Mia handed the backpack over. "Avery, I didn't know Sarah was going to be here. Catherine didn't mention it when she called."

"Right now." She closed her eyes to stop the tears, but she couldn't hold them back. "I don't care." Mia pulled her close, and Avery melted into her arms, holding her tightly. When her tears stopped, she pulled back, and wiped her eyes then blew her nose.

"Feel better?" Mia rubbed her back.

Avery took a few deep breaths. "Yes. They need me right now. All I care about is Catherine and the girls. Sarah and Camden can both go to hell."

Mia smiled and patted her on the shoulder. "See, I was wondering where your fighting spirit had run off to. It's good to see it back. I know you don't like hospitals, but they need you."

She hadn't stepped foot in a hospital since her grandma died a few years ago. Her family waited with her for a week, waiting for her to die. Avery still had nightmares about sitting in her hospital room, watching the rising and falling of her chest as it got shallower and shallower. It came as a great relief when she took her last breath. She died like she lived, with a smile on her face. When she walked out of the hospital that morning, she hoped she would never have to set foot in one for a long while. It was the hardest thing she had ever had to do, watching her die.

"I'll be all right. It's hard, but I'll get through. Even if the only thing that comes out of this is I grow closer to the three of them, I am fine with that. I can't think about anything else right now. All that matters is making sure Lincoln is all right and what kind of recovery she will have."

"Change and get back out there to them. Sarah didn't look pleased when I walked in. I can assume she is having a talk with Catherine about you right now. I'll see you back at home. Don't worry about Polly. I'll take care of her. Change. I'll drop your clothes at the drycleaners."

Avery rolled her eyes. "All right." She grinned when she saw what Mia had packed for her and quickly changed. When she walked out of the stall, she handed Mia her folded clothes. "Thank you."

"Don't mention it. If you need anything call me."

"Okay." What ever happened when she walked back into the waiting room, she would deal with. Catherine needed her right now and Sarah was the least of her problems at the moment. She wouldn't purposely antagonize her, but she wouldn't take any of her shit either. Before heading back to the waiting room, she brushed her teeth, and took a couple of Tylenol. She might have sobered up, but she knew the headache was on its way. With a final internal pep talk, she opened the door and walked out. *She could do this.*

※ ※ ※ ※

When she returned to the waiting room, Camden had left, but Sarah still sat on Catherine's left side and the tension in their small corner of the waiting room had risen a notch. Avery sat down on Catherine's right and set her bag on the floor in front of it. "Have you heard anything yet?"

Abigail grabbed her hand. "No."

"I can't believe you would wear those clothes out in public," Sarah sneered.

Avery looked down at her gray sweatpants and white t-shirt. It might have been plain, but it was designer and better yet, it was comfortable. Avery ignored her and handed Catherine and Abigail each a bottle of water.

"I guess you don't have any manners either?"

Sarah either didn't realize or didn't care that Catherine was barely holding on. Did she not know Catherine at all? "Sarah, I am only going to say this once; shut the hell up. I am here for Catherine and the girls. I don't like you and don't care about your opinions or your feelings. If you want to talk to somebody, talk to somebody else." She pointed around the waiting room.

"Well, I never. Really, Cat, are you going to allow her to talk to me this way?"

Catherine sighed and her fingers shook on her water bottle. "Sarah. Not now."

Before Avery could offer a comeback, a doctor was headed in their direction. Catherine stood up and Avery put her arm around her waist to steady her.

"Lincoln Davenport?"

"I'm her mom."

"Please sit back down." At the alarmed look on Catherine's face, he quickly continued. "Lincoln was very lucky." He waited for everyone to sit down before he went on. "I am Dr. Watson. I'll say again, she was very lucky. We went in and repaired the damage to her right shoulder and arm. She will be in a splint for the next couple of months. There could be some nerve damage, but we won't know more until she wakes up and we can evaluate her. We are looking at a recovery time of at least eight to twelve weeks. She has bruised ribs and a bruised kidney along with numerous other contusions. She has a severe sprain on her left ankle, from where it was pinned underneath the seat in front of her. It's a miracle it wasn't broken. She does have a laceration on her forehead but her CT scan came back clear, as did her MRI. The surgeon that stitched the cut on her forehead said she should only see light scarring after the wound is healed. She has a dozen or so cuts all over her body, but if they stay infection free, I don't see any issues with them. She's probably looking at a week in the hospital than we will reevaluate her and go from there." He grasped Catherine's hand. "Your daughter is very lucky."

Avery let out the breath she was holding and kept a firm grip on Abigail and Catherine's hands. "Thank goodness."

"You call that lucky?" Sarah chimed in.

The doctor cut his eyes to her. "Considering two of the other people in the car didn't make it and the other one is fighting for her life, yes, I would say she was very lucky."

Abigail started shaking next to her so Avery pulled her into her arms. "Can you tell us who didn't make it?"

He regarded his notes. "Her parents told me it was okay to tell you. Tara Crampton and the driver didn't make it."

"Oh God." Catherine's hands flew to her mouth. "She was only fourteen."

"I will tell you the same thing I told her mother. She died on impact. Also, I'm not sure if the police mentioned it, but the driver of the other car didn't make it either."

Avery wrapped her other arm around Catherine's shoulder. "When can we see her?"

"She should be in recovery for another hour or so, then she will be moved to a room."

Catherine accepted the tissue the doctor handed her. "I would like her in a private room if that's possible."

"Of course. I will let them know. Do you have any questions?"

"I should probably set up an appointment with her psychologist?"

"That wouldn't be a bad idea. Normally with survivors of car accidents, they will feel some survivor's guilt. She will need someone to talk to. Also, there is quite a bit of bruising and swelling; please keep that in mind when you see her. We didn't have any issues during surgery, and if infection doesn't set in, I don't see any reason why she shouldn't make a full recovery."

"Thank you. For everything."

He smiled and stood up. "The nurse will let you know when you can see her. Only two adults at a time, but I will allow your daughter to accompany you."

"All right."

After he left, Catherine abruptly stood up. "I

have to use the restroom. I'll be right back." Abigail jumped up and followed her.

Avery sat still, but she could feel Sarah's eyes on her. "What?" she snapped and turned in her direction.

"Don't think I don't know what you're doing."

"I don't really care what you think."

"When Catherine got the call, we were, how do you put it, in a delicate situation."

It took all of Avery's willpower not to snap her neck. "I don't care. The only thing that matters right now is Lincoln and making sure Catherine and Abigail have the support they need."

"She has it," Sarah sneered.

"Not from where I'm sitting. You're being petty and a bitch. Think about them instead of yourself and for once, shut the hell up."

"How dare you." Sarah stood up.

"Oh, I dare."

Catherine and Abigail took that opportunity to walk back in and take their seats. After a drink of water, Catherine looked at Avery then Sarah. "Sarah, sit down. Would you two please be civil to one another?"

"Cat, I don't see what she is doing here anyway." Sarah put her hand on Catherine's shoulder. "She won't be able to come back with us and it's so late she won't be able to see her until tomorrow. She should just go home."

Avery held her breath. If Catherine sent her home now, she would quit tomorrow and never speak to her again. Catherine might be in a relationship with Sarah, but Avery loved Lincoln and didn't want to be anywhere else. At least until she had a chance to see her. Her heart sunk when Catherine turned toward her.

Avery leaned up and whispered in her ear. "If you ask me to leave, this will be the last time you ever see me again." She couldn't read the look in Catherine's eyes and that scared her. Aloud, she said. "I don't have to go back now, but I would like to stay and maybe see Lincoln when she is taken to her room if they'll allow it." Catherine rubbed her eyes, took another swallow of water, then rested back against her seat.

"Cat."

"Sarah, if you want to go, go. Avery will stay with Abigail and me. I know you were supposed to leave today, but cancelled at the last minute. Go get some rest."

"If you're sure." But she was already up and out of her seat. Avery turned her head when she leaned forward and pecked Catherine's lips. Even when Avery knew she was gone, she kept her gaze straight ahead, even though she could feel Catherine's eyes on her.

"I called you three times."

Avery inwardly groaned. "I was mad at you. I thought it had something to do with work."

"You were my first three calls, then I called Mia and Camden."

Avery didn't know what she was supposed to say to that. "Thanks for thinking of me."

She whipped her head around. "Of course I thought of you. I know how close you and Lincoln have grown. Even after this past week, where you have ignored all of us."

Avery ran her fingers through her hair. "I don't want to talk about that. I'm here now and don't plan on going anywhere. In the morning, when you go to see Sarah off, I'll stay here with Lincoln and Abigail."

Catherine looked shocked that Avery would even

suggest such a thing. "I'm not going anywhere."

"I really can't see her coming back here and since your relationship is long distance, I figured you would want to say bye to her. I really didn't mean anything by it and I don't mind staying with the girls."

Catherine frowned. "Our relationship."

"It's not a big deal. I really didn't mean anything about it."

Catherine leaned back in her seat. "I think things have gotten way off track. Don't you?"

"That's why I said we should focus on Lincoln. It sounded like she was going to need a lot of help in the coming weeks."

"Avery, I'm sorry. For everything."

Avery rested her arms on her knees and buried her head in her hands. "You win some, you lose some." She smiled sadly at her and was mindful of Abigail listening to them. "I've only ever wanted you to be happy."

"You stopped sending me flowers?"

"You always got a bigger smile on your face when you received the roses."

"What?"

"It's true. Everybody noticed. I am just glad somebody was able to do that for you, even if it was Sarah."

Catherine shook her head. "Avery, the roses aren't from Sarah."

If they weren't from Sarah, who were they from? "You've had roses delivered once a week for the past month and a half. That's about the time you reconnected with Sarah, wasn't it?"

"Yes, but the roses aren't from her. They are from an old friend. A very dear friend. We meet up again a couple of months ago and talked for the first time in ten years. She was the first person to believe in me. In my talent. Of course it brings a smile to my face. I love her dearly. Her and her husband moved back here a few months ago and when they were settled, she contacted me. She told me she was going to send me a dozen roses, once a week, until fashion week. She's getting older and I adore her."

"That's one of the sweetest things I've ever heard." She felt like a complete ass for assuming. What else had she assumed?

"Why did you stop sending flowers?"

"You told Lincoln the daisies were a sure thing, but when I realized you were already in a relationship, it made me feel like an idiot. Here I was, trying to woo you, and you were already taken. I may not be able to change my feelings toward you, but I would never try and intentionally break you two up. I know my opinion doesn't matter, but you can do a lot better than her." Abigail nodded beside her and Catherine didn't miss it.

Catherine laid her head against Avery's shoulder. "We dated for four years when we were both in our twenties. I thought it would last forever. We parted on good terms and it came as a shock to me when we reconnected. I never meant for any of this to happen. You, her, everything. I have never been good at expressing my feelings. It's hard for me to tell someone how I feel."

"You don't have to do that with Sarah. She already knows you."

"Yes. It's been easy to fall back into that role, though some things are different."

"How could they not be after so many years

apart? I get it. I don't have to like it, but I get it." They both sat up when a nurse informed them to follow her. Abigail grabbed Avery's backpack and slipped it on.

As they walked side by side, Catherine grasped her left hand and Avery held onto Abigail's with her right. "Avery, you don't give yourself nearly enough credit. When we get a bit of free time, we need to talk. Really talk."

"I think that's a good idea."

Abigail clung to Avery's hand as they followed the nurse into a well-lit room. "They are getting her room ready and she should be moved in the next hour or so. You have fifteen minutes." Avery bit back a sob and held Catherine as she leaned against the bed. Abigail let go of her hand, crossed to the other side of Lincoln's bed, and picked up her hand. Lincoln looked so small, hooked up to all the monitors.

"Lincoln," the nurse whispered close to her ear. "You moms and sister are here."

Avery jerked her head up but didn't correct the nurse and neither did Catherine. Lincoln slowly opened her eyes and squinted up at them. "Mom."

Catherine leaned down so she could catch every word. "I'm here, sweetheart. Don't be scared. You're all right. The doctors have taken very good care of you. Don't try and talk." Catherine sniffled. "There will be plenty of time for that later."

"Scary." Lincoln mumbled.

"I know."

"So much blood."

Avery walked around the bed, wrapped her arms around Abigail from behind, and pulled her back against her body. "Really, sweetheart. There were less dramatic ways to get my attention."

Lincoln tried to smile, but it quickly disappeared and a look of pain took its place. "Tara."

Avery hovered above her. "Lincoln." She ran her hand down Lincoln's cheek. "Don't talk. Rest. We're not going anywhere. You're safe here. I promise."

"Linda?" Lincoln grimaced and licked her lips.

Catherine kissed her cheek. "Is alive."

"D...driver?"

Avery and Catherine exchanged looks. "He didn't make it."

"Love me."

"I do." Avery smiled

"Mom too?"

Good grief, even from a hospital bed she was still trying to play matchmaker. "I do." Catherine's eyes widened, but she took Avery's hand across Lincoln's stomach. "Right now, I think it's best if you rest. You should be moved to your room shortly. The more you rest, the quicker you will heal."

"Okay." She was asleep in seconds.

Avery kept one arm around Abigail and her other hand gripped in Catherine's. "She looks so tiny."

"I know." Catherine doubled over and Avery rounded the bed, dragged her in the hall, then pulled her into her arms. The nurse smiled sadly at her over Catherine's shoulder. She clung to her for dear life, and Avery ran her hands up and down her back.

"She's going to be okay. That's what matters. She's a tough kid and with you by her side, she can't fail. Plus, there's me and Abigail." She moved back, pulled a few Kleenexes from the nurses' station, then handed them to Catherine.

"I know I look a mess."

"You're beautiful. I can't think of a single

circumstance where you wouldn't be." Even in this situation, Avery couldn't stop her heart from racing being so close to Catherine. It was a miracle she hadn't already combusted.

Catherine waded the Kleenexes up in her hand and bit her lip before answering. "You'll be here for her?"

"Yes. I'll not abandon her, or you, or Abigail for anything." She interlaced their fingers. "I am not going to put any pressure on you. Especially not now. You deserve so much more than that, but I am here. I just want to let you know that you have options. You know I care about you and if in the end, you don't choose me, I would still like to be a part of Lincoln and Abigail's life. Even though it's taken a bit longer for Abigail to warm up to me, they both mean a lot to me."

She could feel the tears building but blinked them back. The look in Catherine's eyes gave her pause, and after a few moments Catherine let go of her hands, nodded, kissed her on the cheek, then walked back into Lincoln's room. Avery touched the spot Catherine had kissed her, then took a deep breath. It was going to be a long night.

≈≈≈≈

The first couple of days of Lincoln's recovery were hard on everyone. It was difficult to watch her suffering, but true to her word, Avery stayed by her side. After a stern talking to by one of Lincoln's nurses, both she and Catherine went home, took showers, then came back. Avery made sure she grabbed her laptop, so she could still work on her deadlines.

Avery didn't want to gloat and she made a point

not to say 'I told you so', when Sarah did not show up at the hospital again. It came as a great sense of relief when Catherine didn't run to her to say goodbye the day after Lincoln's accident. Avery slumped back on the couch, saved her work, then shut the laptop.

Catherine sat on the bed beside Lincoln, running her fingers through her hair and speaking quietly to her. It wouldn't take much to believe they were a family. The nurses believed they were, and neither Avery nor Catherine had corrected them. Avery knew it wouldn't last, but she was grateful that Catherine agreed no matter what happened with them, she could still have a relationship with Lincoln and Abigail.

Avery groaned when the ringing of Catherine's cell phone shattered the peaceful atmosphere. Over the last few days, she had become quite familiar with Sarah's ringtone and every time it rang, Catherine answered. Avery stood up when Catherine walked to her phone and answered it. Avery drowned out the conversation and sat down on the bed beside Lincoln, who smiled at her. "How are you, kid?"

"I'm alive." She picked at her sheets.

Avery ran her thumb over Lincoln's hand. "That you are and I am very happy about that."

"You and Mom seem to be getting along."

"Lincoln, we both love you."

"I almost died. It would have sucked knowing she choose Sarah over you."

"Stop, please. You did almost die; all this other bullshit can wait." She tapped her on the nose. "You're all that matters right now."

"Sarah, you can't be serious." They both turned toward Catherine, whose voice had steadily been rising. She ran her fingers through her hair, but kept her back to them. "I see. No, no problem. Good. Love you too, bye."

Avery turned her head back toward Lincoln when she squeezed her hand. "I'm all right." That was the biggest lie she had ever told herself, but they both needed to hear it. Having the confirmation of Catherine's feelings from her own lips was a punch to the gut.

"Lincoln," Catherine said. Avery pushed up from the bed, but Catherine waved her back down. "I have to leave for a few hours, but I'll be back later." Avery frowned. Catherine knew Lincoln had a few tests scheduled for that afternoon and she was nervous about them. What could be so important that she would miss them for? She cringed inwardly when Catherine confirmed her assumptions. "Sarah is only in town for tonight and asked if I would meet her for a few hours this afternoon. I agreed, but I will be back later. I promise."

Lincoln narrowed her eyes at her mom. "You won't be here for my tests?"

Avery squeezed her hand. "Lincoln, I'll be here and Abigail will be here once she gets out of her photography class. Let your mom go take care of Sarah and I'll be here when you get back. Maybe I can even get your nurse to bring you some ice cream." She winked.

Lincoln smiled. "I don't think that will be a problem considering she has a crush on you."

Avery took note of the frown on Catherine's face, but didn't care. She had no reason to judge her since she was obviously leaving her daughter to take care of a booty call. "We'll see."

"Mom, go. I know you don't get to see Sarah that often and now that I know Avery is sticking around,

I'm okay."

Catherine cringed, kissed her daughter on the forehead, then pushed the hair out of her eyes. "I won't be long."

"Take your time. Avery is staying."

"Wild horses couldn't drag me away from you." Avery's grin was wiped from her face when Catherine straightened, then kissed her on the forehead before grabbing her purse and leaving the two of them alone.

"I'm sorry," Lincoln said.

"Me too, kid. Me too. Enough about me. How are you really doing?"

"I'm okay. Talking with Dr. English has helped. She's helped me work through some issues. It's still hard, knowing Tara and the driver died and that I won't be able to go to her funeral."

Avery grabbed the Kleenex and handed them to Lincoln, who wiped her eyes. "I know. I talked to Linda's mom and she said she's out of intensive care and stable."

"Everything is so messed up."

"We will deal with things as they come. Day by day."

Lincoln sniffled. "I can't believe Mom left to go be with her."

Avery wondered when she would bring it up and was surprised it wasn't the first thing out of her mouth when her mom had left. Avery tried to be diplomatic. "They don't get to see each other that often." But she shut up with the glare Lincoln sent her way.

"I almost died. Shouldn't I outrank her?"

She should, but she wasn't about to say that, but from the look on Lincoln's face, she knew what she was thinking. "You know what I think?" She hopped off the bed, pulled a chair close, and grabbed the remote. "I think we should watch some mindless TV until they come to take you for your tests."

"Sounds good."

Two hours later, Catherine walked back into the room in a different set of clothes. She looked calm and refreshed. She guessed that's what afternoon sex did to a person. She also looked like a weight had been lifted off her shoulders. Well, damn. Avery kept her eyes on her laptop when Catherine sat down beside her on the couch.

"How long has she been gone?"

Avery eyed the clock. "Almost an hour. She should be back at any time." She debated whether she should tell her or not, but she was her mother. "About thirty minutes after you left, Lincoln had a panic attack and they had to give her something to calm her down." Catherine sucked in a breath beside her and rested her head in her hands. "They would have had to sedate her anyway for the tests; they just had to do it a little earlier."

"I should have been here."

"Yes, you should have." Especially since she saw the fear in Lincoln's eyes when she called out for her mom.

Catherine jerked her head up. "Don't start, Avery."

"You are the one that said you should have been here. I was only agreeing with you." She slammed her laptop closed and stood up. "Tell me, was your meeting with Sarah worth it?"

"Don't act so high and mighty. It's not becoming, Avery."

"Whatever. All I know is that when she called out

for her mom, I was the one that held her hand and comforted her, while her mother was out doing God knows what. She's not stupid; she knows."

Catherine stood up and stalked toward her. "What are you talking about?"

"Please, every time Sarah calls, you jump. Lincoln knew that when Sarah asked, you would run to her."

"You have no idea what you're talking about."

"Give me a break, Catherine. You have different clothes on, you've showered. It doesn't take a rocket scientist to know what you were doing." She waved her hand in front of her. Catherine flinched and took a step back. Avery sighed. "It's none of my business."

"You're right; it's not." She opened her mouth to say something else, but Avery cut her off.

"All I know is that I was here and you weren't. She was scared, Catherine, and it scared me." She swiped at her eyes and looked around the room. She had no reason to be upset with Catherine, none whatsoever. She wasn't hers. She ran her fingers through her hair, feeling the panic take over. She closed her eyes, counted backward from ten, then took several deep breaths to calm herself down, before opening her eyes.

Catherine squinted at her then turned away from her. Catherine wasn't hers and neither was Lincoln or Abigail. She didn't belong here. She gulped several times before striding across the room and shoving her things in her bag. What was she doing here? She stilled and closed her eyes when Catherine's hand rested on hers. She needed to get home.

"I know what you're doing and if you want to leave when Lincoln gets back, I'm sure she'll understand. You could use a good night's sleep, but you promised her you would be here when she got back." Catherine moved her hand, then sat down on the couch. "I had to see Sarah. It was the only chance I would get to until next week. If you would let me explain."

"Stop." Avery put the rest of her things in her bag then sat down beside her. "I'm sorry. Your relationship and what you do with your life on your time isn't any of my business. I shouldn't even be here. I work for you, Catherine, and I will go back to the office tomorrow so things can start getting back to normal. There is a lot to do before fashion week starts next week. I really shouldn't be here."

"Avery—" At that moment, the door opened and Lincoln was being wheeled back in.

The nurse walked over to them when she finished setting Lincoln up. "Everything went well. She's still a bit groggy, but that will wear off in the next hour. I'll come back in about thirty minutes to check on her. Avery," the nurse said and Avery snapped her head up. "I see Catherine went home, showered, and changed. You should do the same. I know it's hard, but I am confident that Lincoln is out of the woods and it wouldn't do for either of her mothers to get sick. You have to take care of yourself."

Avery stood and shook her head. "I'm not sure where everyone got the notion that I'm her mother, but I'm not." The nurse frowned.

"Avery," Catherine said.

"I work for her mother." She kissed Lincoln on the cheek then walked out the door even when Catherine called her name again. She didn't allow the tears to fall until she slumped down in the seat in the back of a cab. It hurt more than she thought possible, but it was time she came to terms with the fact that even though she, Lincoln, and Abigail where friends, she was still only Catherine's employee.

🙢🙢🙠🙠

Avery groaned and rolled over in bed when her alarm blasted beside her. After a quick shower and an even quicker breakfast, she kissed Polly on the head, bid Mia a good day, and headed into work. She stayed home on Sunday and was ready for work when Monday rolled around.

She stopped in the middle of the sidewalk when she noticed three missed calls from Catherine and numerous text messages. She debated about whether to read them, but something could have happened to Lincoln. She decided to read the first one: *Since you're not taking my calls, I figured that maybe a text message would get through. Lincoln was asking about you. She was wondering if you were coming back today. What should I tell her?*

She scrolled down to the last one. *Lincoln's asleep.* She slipped the phone back in her bag and headed up the elevator. Hannah gave her a funny look when she walked in, but Avery headed down the hallway anyway and into the office where everyone continued to give her funny looks. She eyed her outfit, but nothing looked out of place, so she ignored them.

Ten minutes into working, Camden pulled up a chair beside her. "I thought it was just a crush?"

Avery bit her lip. "What do you want? I'm working on the site. Is there something else I should be doing?"

"Avery, I thought we talked about this. I've seen a lot of people come and go through here, and every one of them has had a crush on her." He pointed to

Catherine's empty office. "I like you, and I don't want to see you get hurt. Her and Sarah where here yesterday afternoon. I went looking for Catherine and found them in the closet, kissing. She's taken, Avery. You need to let this little crush go." He stood up without another word and walked back to his desk.

Avery kept her eyes on the screen, and blinked back tears. She couldn't do this. She couldn't. She was in the process of packing her things up when her phone rung. Without bothering to check the caller I.D., she answered it. "Hello."

"You promised you would be here when I woke up on Saturday and I didn't hear from you yesterday. I didn't take you as a liar."

"Actually, Lincoln, I said I would be there when you got back and I was; you were just still asleep."

"Mom looked so sad when I woke up."

"I told her about your panic attack; she was sorry she wasn't there for you." Why was she still defending her?

"I don't think that's what it was. She was sad when she talked about you."

"Lincoln, I take it your mom isn't in the room with you?"

"No."

"Let this go. I am going to. I work for your mom. I am her employee and I realized yesterday that that's all I'll ever be. Your mom doesn't need another friend and she has a girlfriend, but I would still like to spend time with you and your sister. If you want to?"

"I do. I figured we could take another pottery class when I'm completely healed."

"I would love that. I would. I'm going to have to let you go; Camden is glaring at me."

Lincoln sighed. "I'm not really sure if it's my place to tell you or not, because you're acting like an ass. I know your feelings are hurt, but maybe you should have stuck around and talked to Mom yesterday. Maybe then you would have found out that she broke up with Sarah."

Before Avery could comment, Lincoln hung up on her. She sat back and stared off into space. So, she broke up with her. Whatever. She didn't care anymore. She opened a new window and started typing. When her resignation letter was to her liking, she printed it, sealed it in an envelope, and slipped it into her bag. After fashion week, she would give it to Catherine.

She was so caught up in work that she didn't notice someone had stopped in front of her desk until they spoke. She looked up to meet Catherine's ice blue eyes. "My office, now." Without waiting for an answer and expecting Avery to follow, she walked away.

Avery grabbed her notebook and a pen and followed her. Oh, boy.

"Close the door."

That couldn't be good. With a bad feeling settling in her chest, she closed the door, took a seat, and waited for Catherine to talk.

Catherine sat back in her seat and looked out the window. "I don't appreciate the way you spoke to me on Saturday." She held up her hand. "You'll have your chance; let me talk first. But, you were right; I should have been there for Lincoln. After you didn't come back yesterday, she had another mini panic attack. I talked her down, but it occurs to me that she has gotten used to your presence in her life, as has Abigail. They love you." She turned her chair around to face Avery. "I honestly don't know what to do. On one hand, I am going to have to have you in my life, for my girls' sake, on the other hand, I don't know if I can be just your friend. These past few months have taken me by complete surprise. You came into my life and turned it upside down. Then Sarah came back into my life. For the record, I didn't have sex with her yesterday. Lincoln has already informed me that she told you I broke up with her."

"You don't have to explain."

Catherine tapped her finger on her lips. "Oh, I think I do. I met her at a small café and broke things off with her, then I went home, showered, changed, and had a bite to eat before returning to the hospital. What's wrong?"

Why would Camden lie to her? "It's nothing."

"It must be something to put that scowl on your face."

"Camden stopped at my desk this morning and basically told me to get over my crush on you and that you were taken. He said he saw you and Sarah in the closet kissing yesterday."

She pursed her lips. "I see."

"Yes." Avery tried not to fidget, but it was hard not to the way Catherine's eyes on her. What did all this mean?

Catherine leaned forward and pressed a button on her desk. A moment later, Camden's voice floated through, asking if she needed anything. Avery groaned when Catherine asked him to come to her office. They were both quiet until Camden walked in. He sat down beside Avery.

"Camden," Catherine started. "Tell me why you felt the need to lie to Avery and tell her you saw me here, yesterday, kissing Sarah?"

Camden straightened in his seat. "I didn't see what it would hurt. She has a crush on you and it's interfering with her work. You are in a relationship, so I didn't figure any harm would come of it."

Avery stiffened and fought with herself not to knock that smug look off Camden's face. "My work is not suffering."

"Save it, Avery," Camden said. "You walked in here and think just because you have a hard on for the boss that you can do or say anything you please. Just because you sit with her kid in the hospital doesn't mean you'll get a promotion, or even in her pants."

Avery recoiled. "What? That's not." She shook her head. "No."

"Please, don't play dumb; it isn't becoming."

They both jumped in their seats when Catherine slammed her fist on the desktop. "Camden, that's enough. I will not have you speaking to her in that manner. You have no clue what's been going on. Keep your mouth shut or you can leave. There are plenty of women and men who would kill for your job."

Camden jumped up. "You've got to be kidding me. You defend her. You do realize it's been her sending you the flowers and all the little gifts. It's pathetic. We've been taking bets on when she will quit or you fire her because of her stupidity."

"We?" Avery had never heard that tone of Catherine's voice before, but it didn't stop the feeling of humiliation and embarrassment that washed through her at Camden's words.

"All of us have seen the way she looks at you. We knew it was only a matter of time. Let's face it, what could she possibly offer you? Everyone knows you could never fall for someone like her."

"You're right." At her words, Avery's heart completely broke. So, there it was. "I could never fall for someone like her, because I've already fallen."

"What?" Camden spluttered. "What?"

Catherine stood up and crossed her arms across her chest. "I've said I've already fallen." Although she directed her answer to Camden, she never took her eyes off Avery.

Avery blinked a few times, trying to understand what Catherine had just said. Maybe she was having a stroke. She had to be having a stroke. "What?" she said softly.

"Camden, I think it's best if you leave now. Set up a meeting with everyone for tomorrow morning at eleven. You're dismissed. Not another word or you'll be looking for a new place to work." Catherine walked around the desk, then rested back against it in front of Avery's chair. She reached out and tipped Avery's chin up. "Are you okay?" she asked when Camden walked out.

"It's a bit embarrassing to find out everyone has been laughing behind my back. I'm just peachy." She decided to leave Catherine's last comments out.

"I'll deal with them tomorrow. I meant about what I said. I know I've messed up and got caught up in the past. But, I have realized in the last few days how much I rely on you and how much you mean to me. Sarah is my past. I've accepted that now. It was nice to be with someone familiar again. I got sucked into it even though I couldn't get you off my mind." She groaned. "She knew I was always thinking about you. I think that's why she acted out like she did. I'm sorry. I've been such a fool. I hope I haven't ruined everything. I hope it's not too late. Please, Avery, tell me it's not too late?"

Avery stood up and started pacing. What was going on? She stopped abruptly and closed her eyes. Was this really happening? At the touch of Catherine's hand on her arm, she opened her eyes. "Why now? After everything." Her voice cracked.

Catherine licked her lips. "You've been pulling away from us. It scared me. Knowing that you would be so close to me, but it would never be enough." She balled her hands into fists. "Lincoln's accident threw everything into the forefront. Life is short, Avery. I have been holding back. I won't lie, the age difference is a big factor, but I think, if you still want to try, I will play off you for that. You don't seem at all bothered by the difference so I will do my best not to be either."

Avery ran her fingers through her hair. Everything she wanted was standing in front of her. "It hurt, watching you with her." Avery couldn't even bear to say her name.

Catherine swiped at her cheeks. "I'm sorry, darling. So sorry."

Avery reached toward her and wiped the tears from her cheeks. "Don't be sorry. I know you had things to work out and through. I know." She bit back a sob and wasn't sure she should give in so easily, but she knew without a doubt what her answer would be. "I wanted you to come to me. I needed you to be the one to come to me." She grimaced. "Are there any other exes I should be worried about?"

Catherine's smiled and relaxed leaning into Avery's touch. "No. No."

Avery stepped forward and finally did what she had been wanting to for the past few months. She captured the lips she had been dreaming about. She ran her hands down Catherine's back and gripped her ass, pulling her in close. Avery's breath caught in her throat and she leaned into the kiss as Catherine's fingers slipped down her neck, and grabbed the back of her shirt. She deepened the kiss and only pulled away when they both needed air. "Wow." She rested her forehead against Catherine's, who chuckled and kissed her on the cheek. She was exquisite and Avery couldn't wait to explore the rest of her. The emotions swirling in the depths of those blue eyes fascinated her. "I believe there will never be a dull moment with you."

Catherine sighed and pulled Avery closer, snuggling against her chest. "You don't know how happy you've made me and the girls. I have a lot of wooing to catch up on." She kissed Avery's jaw. "I'm sorry it's taken me this long to realize what it was I was feeling and to take a chance on us."

"I love you." She placed her finger over Catherine's lips. "You don't have to say it. Not yet. When you're ready to say it, I will be ready to hear it. I hope you realize that now that I have you, I don't plan on ever letting you go."

Catherine laughed and bit her lip. "Do you promise?"

Avery placed a kiss on Catherine's neck. "I promise. I'm sure Lincoln and Abigail are going to be pretty upset they missed this. They've been trying to get us together for a while."

Catherine grinned, then pulled away from her enough to grab her cell phone that was on the desk and waved it in the air. "They already know. I had to promise them to keep it on speakerphone. I don't think they trusted me on my own. They told me this was too important to mess up. Girls, did you catch everything?"

"Mom, you did awesome. Although we could have done without the kissing," Abigail said.

"I would have liked to have seen Camden fired, but I know you shouldn't do that until after fashion week." Catherine rolled her eyes. "Avery, don't hold anything against Mom for what happened the past few weeks, okay? It just takes some of us longer to reach our final destination. Mom always takes the long way around."

Avery ran her fingers down Catherine's cheek. "I won't, Lincoln. I promise." And she wouldn't. She knew they had a lot to work out, but she was confident this was the first step toward the rest of her life and she was so glad Catherine chose her.

"I told you not to give up," Lincoln stated proudly.

Avery saw her future written in those blue eyes and couldn't wait to see where the road took them. "So you did, Lincoln. So, you did." Catherine ended the call and set the phone back on the desk. "What happens now?"

"Now, you have dinner with us at the hospital and tomorrow night it's just you and me." Catherine's lips were too tempting, so Avery kissed her again.

Avery pulled back and couldn't help the smile plastered on her face. "That sounds fantastic."

"And tomorrow, I think it's time I start wooing you."

※ ※ ※ ※

Avery's nose twitched when a familiar scent invaded her senses. The past two weeks had been amazing between her and Catherine going on a handful of dinner dates, and spending as much time together as possible, but they'd yet to take the next step. A smile broke out on her face when fingertips danced across her cheek, but she remained laying on the couch with her eyes closed.

Lincoln had been released from the hospital two days ago, and had insisted that she was well enough to spend the night at a friend's house and Abigail had agreed. Catherine was skeptical, but after a call to her doctor, he agreed that if Lincoln took it easy, she would be fine. It had been the perfect opportunity for Avery to spend an entire Saturday with Catherine, but she had been called into the office to take care of a few last-minute things. Avery had tried to tag along, but Catherine shot that idea down, telling her she would only be gone for a couple of hours and to relax.

Avery stretched as the fingers resumed their exploration and slowly opened her eyes, spying the clock that hung above the fireplace that read eight o'clock, meaning she had been asleep for three hours. Catherine was sitting on the coffee table in front of the couch and Avery shivered when Catherine's fingers caressed her neck.

Avery groaned and sat up, rubbing her eyes. "I'm sorry, it was not my intention to fall asleep." She ran her fingers through her hair. Catherine stilled her hands and Avery looked up meeting those tempting blue eyes before leaning in and kissing her. When Avery pulled away, she rested their foreheads together. She knew they were taking it slow, but it was getting harder and harder to keep her hands to herself considering how devastatingly sexy Catherine was. Even in a navy tank top, and designer jeans.

"Now, that's what I call a greeting." Catherine

tipped Avery's chin up and kissed her again. This time slowly, exploring every bit of her lips and mouth.

Avery felt like her heart was going to beat out of her chest when they finally pulled apart. "There's more where that came from."

"Cheeky."

Avery tugged on her hand and pulled her down beside her, holding her close, breathing in the scent that was sinfully Catherine. "Get everything straightened out at the office?"

Catherine pulled her arms tighter around Avery's waist. "I did. I would have been here sooner, but I needed to return a few messages. The girls didn't give you any trouble before they left, did they?"

"No, they're good kids." She buried her head against Catherine's neck. "How can I miss you so much when you leave with as much time as we spend together."

"I know the feeling." Catherine laughed and rested her head back on the couch.

Avery took the opportunity presented and kissed her neck, then nipped the spot right below her ear. "At least it's mutual."

"Oh, you can count on that."

When Avery moved in for another kiss, Catherine abruptly pulled away.

"Is something wrong?" Avery scrunched her nose up.

"There is probably something we should talk about."

Avery frowned when Catherine fidgeted. Whatever it was had to be serious, if she was this nervous. Everything had been going well, so she wasn't sure what this was about. "Okay."

Catherine smiled. "It's nothing bad, just something you should be aware of considering where things are headed. As we both know, I am older than you and with that comes certain truths."

"Go on." Avery had a feeling she knew where this was going.

"Avery." Catherine bit her lip. "I am proud of who I am and of what I've accomplished, but, the fact remains, I am still a middle-aged woman who gave birth to twins. My body…It's not easy for me to talk about." Catherine turned her head away, but Avery tilted it back towards her and caressed her cheek.

If she'd known this had been an issue with Catherine, she would have voiced her opinion earlier. She knew Catherine was hesitant about the age difference, but she was always so confident, Avery had no clue this would be a problem. She would do a better job, in the future, of making sure Catherine always knew how much she loved her. "First, you are a remarkable and beautiful woman. Carefree, makeup free Catherine might be my favorite of all. Only the girls and I get to see that side of you. Do you know how special that makes me feel? I can't even describe it." She bit her lip and shook her head. "I am not going to downplay your insecurities, because we all have them. But, please believe me when I tell you that you are everything I want and I love every part of you. Even those parts I haven't seen yet. From my end, you don't have anything to be worried about." She ran her hand down Catherine's cheek. "And I can't wait to explore every inch of you."

Catherine's eyes searched her face. "You really mean that, don't you?"

"I would never lie to you about something that

you're concerned about. I think about you all the time. With and without clothes on. I can tell you one thing. I know the reality is going to be so much sweeter than the fantasy.

Catherine covered Avery's hand and rubbed her thumb across the knuckles. Avery watched the rise and fall of Catherine's chest. Being this close to her always felt right, but it was wreaking havoc on her body. She leaned forward and kissed her again.

Once she was confident Catherine felt comfortable, she intensified the kiss then pulled back and kissed her way down Catherine's jaw and sucked on the spot right below her ear that drove Catherine crazy. Avery pulled back and allowed Catherine to recline on the couch, before things go to heated, and held herself upright above her with hands resting on the cushion behind Catherine's shoulders.

Avery closed her eyes and took several deep breaths as Catherine slipped her hands under her shirt and ran soft fingers along her back. She didn't want to miss a minute of this moment now that it was finally here. Or at least she hoped it was. The kisses were nice, but her body craved so much more. When she opened her eyes, Catherine wrapped her legs around her waist and drew them flush. "Kiss me again, Avery." Catherine wasted no time pulling Avery down and as their lips met, Avery tugged open the button on Catherine's jeans and slipped her hand inside and skimmed her fingertips along the lace she encountered. The kiss wasn't hurried, both content, at the moment, to barely taste one another. Avery shivered as Catherine's fingers danced along her ribs.

"Avery," Catherine said, after a minute, pulling her hands back, and pushing on Avery's shoulders.

"Stop. We have to stop."

Avery frowned, breathless. "What? Why?"

"We were just supposed to have dinner tonight? Do you want to go from dinner to sex? Isn't that moving fast? Weren't we taking things slow?"

Avery shook her head and took a minute to collect her thoughts before answering. "No, it's not moving too fast, but I will only go at the pace that you set. I love you and want you to be comfortable. If kissing is all you want right now, I am more than happy to oblige. I was the one that started this, after all." She smiled, then pecked Catherine on the lips.

Avery pushed herself upright and was moving to get off the couch when Catherine wrapped her arms around her neck to halt her progress. "How did I get so lucky?"

Avery smirked. "Luck had nothing to do with it. It was my exceptional wooing skills."

Catherine smiled that smile that always sent shivers down Avery's spine. "Take me to bed, Avery."

"Are...are you sure?"

"Really, Avery. You know how I hate repeating myself."

"Indeed, I do." She jumped off the couch and pulled Catherine up with her and tightened her arms around her, enjoying the feel of Catherine in her arms. Even holding her it was still hard to believe. After everything they'd been through to get to this moment still felt surreal. "This is really happening, isn't it? Me, you, us, this."

Catherine tucked a loose strand of hair behind Avery's ear. "It's real and there is nowhere else I would rather be and no one else I would rather be with."

They'd only been official for two weeks, and every

day kept getting sweeter and sweeter. Their future would be awesome, but it would have to wait. Right here, right now was all that mattered and Avery would make sure to savor every moment.

Epilogue

Avery sighed and pushed the shaggy mess that had become her hair out of her eyes for the third time that morning. The last six months had been a whirlwind. Not only with Catherine, and their relationship, but also with C.D. Designs and the girls. It had taken a lot of adjustments on everyone's parts. She hadn't even had time to contemplate making an appointment to have her hair cut. She was still on the fence about having it cut at all, especially since Catherine loved to run her fingers through it when they were cuddled together on the couch watching T.V.

The new affordable line had taken off far better than anyone had hoped, not in small part to all the changes she had made to the websites. It had also taken Catherine a few weeks to find a suitable replacement for Camden, but Karen had worked out quite well.

Since that fateful night, she had waited with baited breath for the other shoe to drop. Not because she doubted Catherine's affections for her, but because that's usually how her dating experiences went. Everything seemed too good to be true. Mia and Brady had told her on countless occasions to let her doubts go and just enjoy the journey.

Her love for Catherine grew every day and even though Catherine had yet to say those three little words. She said them every day in her actions but it would be nice to hear them falling from those amazing lips. Her wooing capabilities were out in full force and Avery waited with anticipation of what she would do next.

On the other hand, they had agreed to take things slow. After the entire Sarah debacle, Catherine had made every measure to make sure Avery felt confident in their relationship and Avery loved her even more for it. There wasn't a day that went by that she didn't feel loved and cherished.

She was so lost in her thoughts that it took a moment for her to realize someone had called her name. Lincoln stood in front of her desk, snapped her fingers, then pointed to her mom's office. "She's been calling you for the last couple of minutes." Abigail, who was seated beside Lincoln, rolled her eyes and snickered before going back to her phone.

It was a rocky road for Lincoln, but last month, her doctors had finally cleared her. The only lasting effect from the car accident was a bit of nerve damage to her right arm, and some scars. She had nightmares from time to time, but Catherine and Avery both, along with her weekly visits to Dr. English, were helping her cope with them.

Abigail hadn't come around completely, but Avery had made a dent in their relationship when she designed the Winged Observers new T-shirts and presented them to them one Saturday morning.

Avery jumped up from her desk, gave Lincoln a one-arm hug, winked at Abigail, then walked into Catherine's office. It was a bit odd for both to be in the studio today, but they had both been productive and seemed happy to be there so she didn't think too much about it. Avery eyed the walls of the office and couldn't help but feel a sense of peace and contentment when she spied the half dozen or so photographs that had been added to the walls since she and Catherine started dating. Brady took her favorite at another Harry Potter weekend that was held at Catherine's townhouse. They were all dressed up, Polly sat on the ground in front of them, and Abigail was holding Digger. The smile on her face and the look Catherine directed her way instead of the cameras told anyone looking at the photo everything they needed to know.

Avery felt her heart flutter when she took in the woman she loved sitting behind her desk. That morning she had the pleasure of watching Catherine dress in that black Chanel skirt and cream colored, silk top she had on. On more than one occasion, she had to remind herself to breathe whenever she was around the other woman. Catherine smirked, crooked her finger, then pointed to the corner of her desk. She reached up to take her glasses off, but Avery stilled her with a shake of her head. Catherine arched her eyebrow.

"Keep them on," Avery said.

"And why is that?" Catherine grinned, already knowing the answer.

Avery ran her finger along Catherine's jaw line. "Because they ratchet your sexiness to a whole other level."

"Very well." Catherine grabbed Avery's wandering hand and kissed the palm. "I have an idea that will launch our social media presence skyward. In fact, I've been thinking about it for a while now."

Avery noticed a slight tensing of Catherine's shoulders but quickly set her unease in the background. "What's your idea?"

It took her several minutes to answer and when she did, Avery had to ask her to repeat it three times. "I said, announcing Catherine Davenport's engagement would do the trick, wouldn't it?"

Avery sat dumbfounded, not quite believing what her ears where hearing. "Engagement?" She squeaked. Catherine's grin set her heart racing.

Catherine grasped Avery's hands between hers. "Avery, I love you. I think I have from the moment you walked through my office door. Do you have any idea how good your ass looked in those Carolina Herrera trousers?" She smiled. "These last few months have been amazing and only solidified my feelings for you and your place in my life. In our lives."

She had said those three words and had completely thrown Avery's whole world out of alignment at the same time. "Wait. I thought you wanted to take things slow?" If Catherine asked, she would say yes, but she had to understand where Catherine's reasoning first.

Catherine waved her hand in the air. "I believe we have been taking it slow. I've known you for almost a year. You love me, my girls, and Digger, and we love you and Polly. What more could any of us want? It's the right time. It is getting harder and harder to come home at night and not have you there with us. I thought a lot about just asking you to move in with us, because you pretty much already have, but we discussed it and all three of us felt this was the better solution. I have waited a long time to get married. Deep down, I knew when I finally did, it would be for keeps. Do you understand? This isn't a whim on my part, Avery. This is it. You are it. Our life together will be spectacular. Avery Michaels, will you marry me?"

Catherine picked up a small box from the corner of the desk that Avery hadn't even noticed when she walked in, and opened it. Nestled inside was a gorgeous four-carat Princess Cut Infinity Twist diamond engagement ring set in platinum. Avery's heart was pounding in her chest and she took a deep breath to ground herself or she was likely to pass out. She didn't have to look to know the girls would be standing in the doorway. Now she knew why they had both came into the studio with Catherine that morning. They obviously planned this together.

Was it too soon? What if everything went south? What if next week she woke up and it was all a dream? What if Catherine was a dream? She bit her lip and melted into Catherine's eyes, which held only love, trust, and commitment. This was crazy, but she didn't care. She knew what it was like to live without Catherine and what it was like to live with her. All she cared about was the woman waiting anxiously in front of her.

She leaned forward and planted a chaste kiss on her lover's lips at the same time Catherine slipped the ring on her finger. She laughed and fell into Catherine's lap, wrapping her arms around her neck, and kissing her on the cheek. She smelled amazing and felt like home. Catherine tightened her arms around her waist and waved her girls over. Avery kissed her neck once more, then whispered in her ear. "What will I wear?"

About the Author

Born near Chicago, but raised in Southern Illinois, where she still lives, Shannon spends her free time writing. When she isn't writing, she enjoys binge watching fantasy, science fiction, or true crime shows.

You can contact Shannon at -

Website: smhfiction.com
Email: smh1981@live.com
Facebook: facebook.com/smharrisauthor
Twitter: @smhfiction

Check out Shannon's other books.

The Adearian Chronicles - Book One - The Oath –
ISBN – 978-1-943353-17-0

Ex-mercenary, Lanis Welsh, is finally at a place in her life where she is content with what and who she is; High Priestess Anya's Protector and Lover. After an unexpected request, she has no choice but to leave Anya's protection in the hands of someone else and travel back to the one place that holds nothing but bad memories. When she is manipulated into signing an oath she has no desire to fulfill, she questions the very truths she has built her life on. As strangers become friends and enemies become allies, Lanis must face the demons from her past. It doesn't take her long to realize there is more going on than anyone could have ever foreseen and nothing and no one can be trusted.

Adearian Chronicles - Book 2 – Revelations – ISBN - 978-1-943353-33-0

What would you do if you were faced with finding and saving the one person who held your heart, but you only had two weeks to do it?

When the unexpected happens and Lanis's world is turned upside down, her and Elson have no choice but to align themselves with two people from a strange land. With new enemies at play, and a Goddess that seems to have forsaken them, Lanis relies on the only people she can; her friends. To fight the demons that plague her daily, she has to separate her love for Anya, from the task she must perform. On top of the unknowns, she is gifted a small black book that changes the way she sees everything and everyone around her. As her world starts to crumble, Lanis must face her fears and the nightmares that invade her dreams. With the hours ticking away, she must come to terms with the fact that she might already be too late.

www.ingramcontent.com/pod-product-compliance
Lightning Source LLC
LaVergne TN
LVHW040056080526
838202LV00045B/3657